I'M FOREVER YOURS

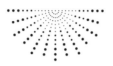

KATHLEEN BALL

Copyright © 2018 by Kathleen Ball

All rights reserved.

No part of this book may be reproduced in any form or by any electronic or
mechanical means, including information storage and retrieval systems,
without written permission from the author, except for the use of brief
quotations in a book review.

❧ Created with Vellum

CHAPTER ONE

The wind kicked up, and dust swirled around Lee Ann Simpson as she stood at the Big M Ranch gates and waved to Walter Hives. He'd been kind enough to give her a ride from the bus stop to the ranch. And now she hesitated outside the gate. She'd left two years ago on such a high note of making it big as a writer for a popular magazine. Now her spirit was crushed, and the thought of returning as a failure overwhelmed her.

But she had nowhere else to go. Her daddy was the foreman on the Marlboro ranch, and all she wanted was a big hug from him. She hadn't been the best at staying in touch. In fact, the last time she talked to him was over three months ago.

Gathering her courage and taking a deep breath, she opened the gate and entered then closed it behind her. The driveway to the big house was long, lined with plenty of pastures that were dotted with outlying buildings. She passed two barns a house and a few trailers. She'd grown up here, and for the first time in weeks, her tension eased. She felt safe.

The weather was hotter in Fort Worth than San Antonio. Sweat formed on her brow as she carried her suitcase to the foreman's house. She opened the door and stopped in her tracks, dismayed.

Why was the furniture covered with sheets? Where was her father? A lot of his books and other personal things were still scattered in familiar places about the room, so what had happened?

She had to find out. Grabbing her case, she headed to the big house.

The door swung open before she reached the front porch, and she found herself in a big hug from the housekeeper, Agnes.

"You sure are a sight for sore eyes. I kept praying you'd come home, but your dad said you were busy."

Lee Ann took a step back with her mouth hanging open. "What do you mean I was too busy? He never called me."

Agnes raised her right brow. "I was there when Gunther himself called. He left a message that it was important you call back."

Lee Ann shook her head. "I never got the message. Where's my dad?"

"He's here. We decided not to send him to hospice. We have a nurse living here instead."

The breath whooshed from her lungs as if she'd been gut-punched. "Hospice? I need to see him."

Agnes nodded. "Of course, honey. Let's go inside."

She'd thought she packed light but the suitcase became heavier each time she had to pick it up. Her arm and ribs still bothered her, and she had to fight to keep from dropping her luggage and rubbing the pain away as she followed Agnes into the house.

"Well, look who finally decided to make an appearance," Gunther Marlboro drawled, leaning back against the kitchen counter as he looked her up and down. He hadn't changed any. Still too handsome for his own good and just as cocky. He did have a few worry lines on his forehead that hadn't been there two years ago, but he still wore his dark hair short.

His blue eyes glowered at her, and ice formed in her veins.

"I didn't know Daddy was sick." It sounded lame even to Lee Ann. She drew a deep breath. "I'd like to see him if you don't mind."

Gunther crossed his massive arms in front of him. "Actually, I do mind. You've treated him shabbily since you left." Their gazes warred silently for a moment, and then he sighed and dropped his arms. "But I know he wants to see you. We converted the living room into his room and I had a new bathroom with a walk in shower put in for him."

Gunther made no move to escort Lee Ann, so she nodded and strode down the hall to the living room on her own. The sight that greeted her tied her stomach into knots. Surely this frail creature couldn't be her father. Where was the strong and hearty man she'd known her whole life? His chiseled face was now thin and drawn. Multiple IVs were hooked up, one in his arm, one near his neck. A heart monitor beep-beeped an erratic rhythm. His gray pallor scared her.

Swallowing hard, she took a step toward him then another. He'd always been such a strong robust man, and it hurt her heart to see him like this. His eyes were closed, but the rise and fall of his chest and the beeping heart monitor told her that he was alive. How had this happened? Why hadn't he called her?

"Daddy? It's me. It's Lee Ann." She took his hand in hers. It was cold as ice.

His eyelashes fluttered a few times before he finally opened his eyes. "Is that you, my baby girl? I've been holding on until I could see you again. It's been so long. I left messages. You need a cell phone."

She glanced away. She had a cell but used it only for work. "I'm so sorry, Daddy. I didn't get any messages, but I'm here now."

"How long can you stay? I bet you need to get back to San Antonio and your job."

She shook her head. "I've come back home, Daddy. The big city no longer appeals to me. I'll find a job and apartment closer to here."

"You'll stay here with me." His voice was becoming hoarse.

"Daddy, I don't think Gunther will want me around. But don't worry about me."

He squeezed her hand. "I'm going to nap for a bit. Will I see you later?"

She summoned up a smile. "Of course you will. I love you, Daddy."

"I love you too, baby girl." He closed his eyes.

Tears threatened as she left the room. She hurried and grabbed her suitcase, hoping to leave before having to face Gunther again. But to her dismay, he stood blocking the door.

"We need to talk, and you don't look so good. Agnes is making us some lunch. Why don't we sit out back and eat."

"I suppose we do need to talk." She followed him to the back of the house. It always amazed her that he had outside fans in his big gazebo. She'd loved sneaking away there to read when she was a kid.

"The place looks good."

"Not too much changes around here. Have a seat." He gestured to the table in the middle of the gazebo. As soon as she sat down, Agnes was there serving them sweet tea.

Sweat instantly beaded on the glass, and Lee Ann touched

it with her forefinger. "Thank you, Agnes. You can't find tea like you make anywhere else."

"You're sweet, Lee Ann. I'll have lunch ready in a bit."

As soon as Agnes was out of earshot, Gunther turned toward her. "Why didn't you return any of our calls? We had no way to get in touch with you personally. For the love of Mike, why didn't you have a phone or at least a cell? Why didn't you try to call your father? What type of daughter are you?" His voice became louder with each question.

"What happened? How'd he get to be so sick?"

Gunther sighed. "He had a stroke about a year ago."

Lee Ann closed her eyes and swallowed hard. "Why didn't he tell me?"

"He didn't want you to feel as though you had to come home. I wanted to tell you, but he made me promise. Honestly, I thought you'd at least be home for Christmas. He was recovering from the stroke, able to live alone and was regaining his strength." He sighed heavily. "But then three weeks ago, he passed out and we called the ambulance. Honey, he has lung cancer and it was caught too late."

A chill ran up her spine as she cringed. "Oh no. I wish I never left."

"We, uh...finally tried calling your work number."

Heat bloomed in her cheeks. "I had some difficulty with a coworker, and I wasn't getting my messages. I had to quit and I thought to come home, but home isn't here anymore." Fatigue and despair settled over her. She'd been fighting for over three months and she was played out.

"So your big city job didn't pan out? I thought you were going to be famous." The sarcasm in his voice was too much. She clasped her hands to keep from falling apart.

"Not everything works out the way you imagine. I grew up very sheltered and I thought people to be honest and decent." A sad laugh slipped out. "They aren't. I found out the hard way and now I'm back but don't worry. I won't be your problem. I saved enough money to pay rent while I look for a job. I want to stay close for my dad." Looking down at her hands, she could feel his warm gaze on her, and she barely squeezed out her request. "Will you let me use your computer to see if there are any apartments to rent?"

"Why don't you stay here for a while? I think it would ease your father's mind."

She shook her head. "Thank you, but I can't. You, yourself, said I was never destined to live in such a fine house. I can just go to town if you don't want me to use your computer."

The silence stretched until she glanced up at him. She didn't like the way he was studying her as though he was trying to figure out what was wrong.

"Stay in the foreman's house," he finally suggested. "You can work on the ranch. Woody is in charge for now. I would like it if you had dinner with us each night. Now's the time to spend your days with your father. He's alert a good part of the time, and I'm sure he'd love your company." He paused, one eyebrow quirked upward. "Deal?"

She released a sigh and got to her feet. "Deal. I'm really not very hungry. If you don't mind, I'd like to go to Dad's place and take a shower then come back and spend time with him."

He nodded. "Go, your dad will enjoy spending time with you." He followed her to the front door.

She reached down to grab her bag again and winced in pain.

"What happened? You move like you've been kicked by a horse."

"I slipped in the shower," she mumbled, lifting the bag. "You must remember me being clumsy. I'll be back in a bit."

GUNTHER WATCHED her walk across the yard. He should have carried her bag for her, but he was stunned by her slipping in the shower excuse. Lee Ann was as agile and graceful as they came. She'd never been the clumsy type. She had shadows hidden in her big blue eyes. He'd caught a flash of them here and there. Something wasn't right.

Shaking his head, he pinched the bridge of his nose and put a halt to his pondering. He had a full plate, and he couldn't add her problems to it.

James was dying and that was slowly ripping his heart out. He'd been able to counter his grief with his anger against Lee Ann for not caring. But apparently, that hadn't been the case, and now he felt off kilter, with no place he could direct his anger of the situation.

He was also trying to buy a tract of land from Felicia, the niece of the property's previous owner. For some reason, she thought it was worth much more than it actually was. Her head was full of big ranches and big money. Maybe she watched too much television or something. He'd have to wait her out, but it was as frustrating as all get out.

"She left?" Agnes asked with a salad plate in each hand.

"She wasn't hungry, and she wanted to get cleaned up."

"It's nice to have her back, don't you think?" Agnes smiled.

He shook his head. "Agnes, don't get your head full of matchmaking ideas. She can't stand me anyway."

"We'll see." She handed him his plate. "Your burger will be ready in a few minutes. Don't forget Felicia is coming to dinner tonight. Did you want me to serve anything special?"

He frowned. "That's tonight? No, in fact stew with corn-bread would be best. Don't use any of the good china or anything. You don't have plates with chips in them do you?"

Agnes laughed. "No, but I do have some fancy paper plates and plastic utensils. That little gal will be disappointed. She thinks you're rich and can provide her a life of leisure."

"I'm going to dispel her of that notion."

Agnes walked to the back door and held it open. "Go eat your salad. I'll bring your burger out. It sure is nice to have Lee Ann back. I've missed her."

Gunther sat and ate but, eating outside had lost its appeal when Lee Ann left. At least she'd be there for dinner tonight. Maybe she could listen to Felicia chatter on and on. Whatever had happened to making land deals with a handshake or even going through a lawyer? He'd never had to practically date a woman to make a deal. Then again, she was from up north and didn't know Texas at all.

He brought his empty plates in and set them on the kitchen counter. He settled his Stetson on his head and walked toward the door. Time to put in some ranch work. In the hall, he passed Lee Ann heading back in to see her father. They smiled at each other.

The sweet, clean smell of her had him thinking about her hours later while he drove cattle from one pasture to another. He didn't like perfume much, but he liked the way Lee Ann smelled.

A steer bumped him. Dang, she had him distracted already. No, he had to remember she hated the ranch and she thought herself too good to live on it. He'd never been so disappointed in his life as when she'd told him her plans to move to San Antonio. She'd had stars in her eyes, and they hadn't been for him.

He spurred his quarter horse to go after a stray steer. The stars were all gone. What had happened in San Antonio? Once the steer had been guided back into the group, he relaxed in his saddle and stared at the sea of cattle. She'd crushed him when she left and she didn't even know.

"Boss, are you coming in?" Woody asked, interrupting Gunther's musings.

Gunther grinned. "Hot date you need to get to?"

"You know it. Want to come?"

"On your date? Heck no."

Woody laughed. "I meant to the Full Holster Saloon. You might get lucky."

"I can do you one better. I have two women coming to dinner tonight."

"Spill the details. What are you waiting for?"

Gunther chuckled. "The lovely and annoying Felicia will be attending as well as Lee Ann."

Woody's smile vanished. "So, she's back. Did she say why she didn't bother to come home to see her father?" The anger in his voice surprised Gunther.

"She hasn't said much. Something happened in San Antonio. She isn't the same bubbly girl we knew. I'm just glad she's back for James' sake. Have a good night." He watched Woody ride across the ranch. It was time to go home, but he didn't want to. Being a responsible adult had many drawbacks.

LEE ANN WATCHED as her father's nurse helped him to eat. Shelly was a nice woman with great nurturing skills. Lee Ann had liked her from the moment they met. She always had a smile on her face, and her father really seemed to enjoy her.

She'd berated herself all through her shower about being a terrible daughter. She should have called but the trouble she'd been having with her boss had overwhelmed her. Still she should have called. She'd had a good cry, though, and now it was time to smile for her dad.

"You being here is helping," Shelly said. "He has his color back in his face. I think I saw a twinkle in his eye."

"You're the one who takes excellent care for him. I can't thank you enough."

"My pleasure."

"Dad, I'll be back in a bit. I'm having dinner with Gunther."

Her father smiled. "And Felicia."

"Who's Felicia?"

"Some barracuda who is trying to get her hooks into Gunther. Have fun!"

Lee Ann chuckled and shook her head. "It sounds like a delightful time." She stopped in the restroom and checked her face. After dabbing on a bit of lip-gloss, she straightened her shoulders and walked down the hall. It was bad enough to have to spend time with Gunther and his piercing stare, but she wasn't in the mood for a barracuda.

She walked into the family room and immediately felt outclassed. Felicia was a lovely, petite, brunette with deep brown eyes. She was attractively dressed in a low-cut designer dress. Gunther looked handsome in his jeans and plaid shirt. Her jeans with a hole at the knee and her plain purple t-shirt didn't quite measure up.

While Lee Ann wore only lip-gloss, Felicia was beautifully made up. There was no denying her sophistication. Lee Ann had met plenty of women like her in San Antonio, and she knew she always paled in comparison.

Putting on her best smile, she greeted Gunther, who immediately stood and introduced her to Felicia.

"We can wait for you to change if you like," Felicia said. No hello, just a direct hit against Lee Ann.

"I wouldn't dream of it. We're family here and this is how we've dressed for dinner for as long as I can remember." She sat on a floral chair across from Felicia.

"May I offer either of you two ladies a drink?" Gunther asked.

Felicia perked up. "I'd love some scotch."

"Lee Ann?"

"No, thank you. I'm not much of a drinker."

Gunther nodded and poured Felicia her drink, handed it to her and sat down.

"You're not having a drink either, Gunther?" Felicia asked. "You usually do."

"Enjoy yours. I'll probably have wine with dinner."

"I was wondering, do you have your own wine cellar?" Felicia leaned forward waiting for the answer.

Lee Ann tried to keep from smiling but it didn't work.

"No, I don't. I wouldn't do it justice if I had one. I can't afford the luxury of expensive wine. We have a few wineries close by, and I buy from them. I like to keep as local as I can. Support the local economy and all."

"So, Lee Ann how long have you known Gunther?" Felicia wore an *I don't really care but I'm being polite* smile on her face.

"We've been together forever. He was my first kiss. I've been away on business for a bit but I'm home now." Lee Ann sat back and crossed her ankles. She was enjoying the look of shock on Gunther's face and the one of annoyance on Felicia's.

"Dinner is ready!" Agnes called.

Lee Ann and Gunther stood but Felicia put her hand out waiting to be helped up. So, Felicia was a helpless one. Good! Gunther didn't like helpless females.

Agnes led them into the kitchen and gestured for them to sit at the ancient, scarred wooden table. Lee Ann made sure not to sit in the chair that had uneven legs. The confused look on Felicia's face as her chair wobbled back and forth was priceless.

"Hope you don't mind eating in the kitchen but this is

what we usually do. I figured since you've been here a couple times already, Felicia, we could forego formality. The stew is on the stove and I cut the cornbread for you. I have a quilting party to attend. I'd appreciate it if y'all pitched in and cleaned the kitchen." Agnes grabbed her purse and walked out the door but not before Lee Ann saw the humor in her eyes.

"You really eat in the kitchen?" Felicia's disdain was palpable.

Gunther nodded. "If you want some stew, help yourself. I'll open a bottle of wine."

Felicia got up and filled her bowl with stew and took a small plate and put cornbread on it.

Lee Ann followed behind grabbing two of everything. One for her and one for Gunther. She was rewarded with a smile when Gunther returned with an open bottle of red wine. He grabbed some paper cups and poured some wine into one.

"Here ya go, Felicia. Lee Ann, would you like some?"

"I'm fine. I'm just going to have some water."

Gunther raised his right brow as he stared at her. Maybe he thought she was pregnant or something, but that wasn't the reason she didn't drink anymore.

She filled her paper cup with water, sat at the table, and picked up the plastic spoon.

"Dig in." Lee Ann suppressed a laugh at the wide-eyed look she got from Felicia. Gunther shot her a surprised but pleased look.

Felicia gripped her plastic spoon and picked through the stew, eyeing it warily. She gulped down some wine and took a bite of the meat. It looked as though she relaxed a bit.

"How's the wine?" Lee Ann asked her. A wine cellar, indeed. The way she gulped it down, she had no appreciation for fine wine.

"It's very good for local wine. A fine bouquet, I'd have to say. Don't you agree, Gunther?"

Gunther glanced at Lee Ann as though looking for a clue as to what they were talking about.

"Local wines are surprisingly good," Lee Ann volunteered.

"Oh, yes." Gunther nodded. "I have a few best friends who own wineries. They've won many awards."

"I'd love to go with you," Felicia said, her eyes shining.

Gunther furrowed his brow. "To where?"

Felicia sighed loudly. "To the winery of course. You work too hard. I bet you're thinking about work right now instead of enjoying a nice dinner with us."

He took a sip of his wine and nodded. "I do have a few things on my mind. Mostly Lee Ann's father. He's been a close friend for years. I'm glad you're back, Lee Ann. Your father actually smiled at me when I checked on him a little bit ago."

"It's funny how fast life can change. One day everything is fine and then the next…Thanks for letting me stay in the foreman's house. I really appreciate it though it rightfully belongs to Woody now." Lee Ann had been raised to be a strong self-reliant woman. Lately all she wanted to do was curl up in a ball and cry. She kept everything bottled up and there were days she felt as though she'd just explode at any second.

"This is your home, Lee Ann." His voice was soft and full of concern. She wasn't used to that from him.

"Maybe I should just move into that old shack of my uncle's and we could all be neighbors," Felicia broke in, her voice somewhat brittle.

"Mooney was your uncle? What a sweet man. He once caught me stealing eggs from his henhouse." Lee Ann paused and smiled. "He took me into his house and made me help fix breakfast. We had scrambled eggs and bacon."

Gunther laughed loudly. "Remember the time I dared you to ride one of the hogs?"

She gave him a look of mock outrage. "Yes I do and I remember the bruises I ended up with and the lecture we both got from my daddy." She wagged her finger at him. "You tried to lead me astray. I don't know how many times I was told I wasn't allowed to hang out with you ever again."

Felicia cleared her throat. "I didn't know you too are close in age. You still look like a teenager, Lee Ann."

Gunther gazed at Lee Ann and smiled. "She does, doesn't she? I'm five years older, but she could always keep up with me. She could also run faster, climb trees higher, and beat me in any horse race. I did beat her at fishing though." His smile widened into a grin. "She doesn't like worms."

Warmth flooded Lee Ann, and she bet her face was red. "A lot of people don't like worms." She gazed into his blue eyes and smiled. "We sure did have fun."

A giant frown creased Felicia's forehead. "I'm surprised you ever left, Lee Ann. Your childhood sounds like one of those stories that ends in marriage." Felicia then tilted her head and smiled a bit too sweetly.

She knew. Felicia knew why Lee Ann had left and was playing stupid.

Lee Ann shrugged. "I got a job offer in San Antonio from All in One Magazine. I started out getting coffee for everyone but after a year or so I moved up to writer."

Gunther stared at her. "I didn't know they published you."

"Yes. Well the first one was a poll. It was the bikini verses the tankini. I was surprised that most women prefer a little more coverage than a bikini provides."

"Isn't that cute, Gunther?" Felicia's voice cut in. "A poll, imagine that."

Gunther shot Felicia a look of annoyance before he grinned at Lee Ann. "That's real good, honey. I know you worked hard." He pushed back from the table. "I expect you want to visit with your dad. I have a ton of paperwork. Felicia would you mind cleaning up before you leave?"

It took everything within her not to laugh at the expression on Felicia's face. Felicia looked like a mad hen.

"Thanks, Felicia." Lee Ann left the kitchen in a hurry. As she walked down the hall to her dad's room, she smiled at the great memories she'd just shared with Gunther. Her nostalgic happiness faded along with her smile as she remembered when she'd left. And why.

GUNTHER SAT at his desk in his office. It was a big room with oversized furniture and books everywhere. His great grandfather had built the house. There had been many improvements over the years but it was the same desk he'd used that Gunther now sat behind. He'd never realized how big their shoulders must have been to bear the responsibility of it all.

Gunther gazed across the room to the big aging map that hung over the fireplace. Through the years, many parcels had been added to the ranch and they were all added to the map. There had been many hard times but they persevered.

The door opened, and Felicia walked in without knocking. That was a pet peeve of Gunther's. Common courtesy dictated that a person should knock first.

"All done?" he asked.

She nodded and then took a seat in one of the plush chairs in front of his desk. "You're welcome. I have to admit I don't usually do my own cleaning." Her face wrinkled in distaste. "I have people for that."

"I have Agnes. This is a working ranch, and everyone is expected to pitch in and pull their own weight."

"I see. What is Lee Ann's job while she's here, or is she paying her way with certain favors?"

And there was pet peeve number two: judging a person's character. "I'm not naïve, but you certainly don't mean to imply..."

Irritation flashed in her eyes, and she shook her head. "Don't bother denying it. I saw how you two looked at each other. You're intimately involved. Is it a temporary arrangement?"

Gunther saw movement at the doorway, and he inwardly groaned when he realized Lee Ann was standing there.

She strode into his office and faced Felicia. "I am not, nor have I ever repaid any debts or favors by sleeping with anyone. I don't understand women like you. If I have something or do a better job, you instantly jump to the conclusion that I'm hopping into bed with some man. I work to make my way, and I work hard. While everyone else assumes there are shortcuts in life, I know there aren't. I also know that you can only rely on yourself. If you don't you'll wake up someday betrayed, wondering what to do next." She stormed from the room.

Felicia stared at the door, one brow lifted in feigned shock. "I guess I made her mad."

"You did, Felicia. Good night. I'm sure you can show yourself out." Gunther looked down at the paperwork in front of him then brought his gaze back up to meet Felicia's. "Oh, and I don't want the property anymore. The price is becoming too high."

Her jaw dropped and she stared at him. Then she stood and gave him a glare before she left.

He wasn't sure how to deal with her stubbornness. Hopefully if he didn't act as though he wanted the property she'd want to sell.

CHAPTER TWO

*G*unther leaned against his front porch railing drinking his third cup of morning coffee. He hadn't slept well since Lee Ann had returned three days ago. Ever since dinner with Felicia, she'd made excuses not to eat dinner with him. She'd been to the house plenty...when he wasn't there.

Sweat already beaded on his forehead. It was going to be a hot one. That was the only thing he didn't appreciate about Texas, the heat.

He'd stuck around the house a bit later than usual, hoping to catch a glimpse of Lee Ann but she hadn't come out of the foreman's house yet.

Her speech in his office played and replayed in his head. He understood a bit of it, but something much larger had happened to her. He didn't have a clue to what, but he felt in his gut it was bad. And he needed to know what it was; he felt that in his gut also. He should call the magazine and see what he could find out. Better yet, he had a detective friend in San Antonio, Andy Morellis.

Before he had a chance to go inside he spotted Woody walking his way. "Morning!"

"Morning, boss." Woody walked up the three steps to the porch and took off his Stetson. "We have a problem. Well not exactly a problem, but—"

Gunther shook his head. "You are too long-winded, Woody. Spit it out."

"Lee Ann is chopping wood. I told her it wasn't something she needed to do, but she paid me no heed. She swings that ax like pro, but she looks like she's in pain with each swing."

Gunther put his cup down on the porch table. "I'll deal with it. Thanks, Woody." He grabbed his hat and headed over to the side of the barn.

There she was, and Woody was right, she was in pain. He waited until she finished chopping the piece she had up on the block before he walked over to her. He gently took the axe from her and cursed when he saw that she wasn't wearing gloves. Taking a deep breath, he took her hands in his and looked at her palms. She'd broken the skin in multiple places, and they were both bloody.

"Let's go to your house and get you cleaned up." He waited, but she didn't protest. She just followed him.

He led her into the kitchen and had her sit down. Her face was drawn and she had a look of defeat. He found a cloth and wet it. Sitting next to her, he took one of her hands and gently wiped away the blood. Then he did the same to the other. She didn't say a word the whole time but she occasionally stiffened and caught her breath.

He took another cloth and wiped the sweat off her brow. The unshed tears in her eyes hurt his heart. She moved her body slightly and winced. Gingerly, she put a hand on her torso.

Slowly he knelt in front of her and lifted up her T-shirt.

"Why didn't you tell me?" He gently touched her black and blue skin. "How the heck were you able to lift that ax? Are you crazy?"

A lone tear rolled down her face. "I think I may very well be crazy."

"Have you seen a doctor?" He stood and slowly lifted her into his arms. He carried her to her bed and laid her on it. "I'm going to call the doctor."

"No!"

"This isn't up for discussion. Lee Ann, you must be in horrible pain." A frown pinched his brow. "Who did this? I think we need to call the police."

She grabbed his arm. "No, no police. Please, Gunther just leave it alone. It won't end well."

He sat on the bed next to her. "Are there more bruises?"

She nodded and he had to bite his tongue not to swear.

"Maybe you could send Shelly over when she's not busy with Daddy. I don't want to be any trouble."

"No more chopping wood?"

She shook her head. "No more chopping wood. I haven't been sleeping, and I thought if I tired out my body "

He sighed. "Will you at least tell me what happened?"

She turned her face away from him. "Not now. I just can't. I thought I could just brave it out and no one would ever know, but I should have known you would figure it out."

"All right, honey. I'll send Shelly over. You rest for a bit." He reached out, intending to stroke the side of her face, but she practically jumped out of her skin.

Rage filled him, threatened to pour out, and he got up. He'd been mad as hell when he had seen the bruises, but now it was much worse than that. Someone had beat the tar out of her. And cringing at his touch... Had she been raped? He left her house and took two steps before he had to stop and take a breath. She seemed so uncharacteristically defeated.

Why wasn't she spitting mad? Damn, it probably hadn't been the first time. It took everything he had not to find something to punch. He didn't want to scare her and punching an inanimate object, he'd be bound to have bloody knuckles.

***

LEE ANN numbly sat up in her bed. She'd been washed, plastered in ointment, bandaged, and questioned by both Shelly and Agnes. She said as little as possible. They asked if she'd been raped and she honestly answered no. Shelly made a call to a doctor, and he called in a prescription for pain. Shelly must have some connections. It was hard to get painkillers.

Gunther was waiting in the family room, and she dreaded seeing him. She feared the questions she wouldn't answer. There had been too many threats against her father and Gunther; she couldn't take the chance.

The door opened, and she tried to harden her heart. She didn't want to shed any tears. The concern on Gunther's face when he crossed the threshold was almost her undoing, but she bit the side of her cheek. For some reason it usually kept her tears at bay.

He carried a chair into the room and put it next to her bed, scanning her from head to toe before he sat down. "Are you okay?"

"I will be. Thank you for sending Shelly and Agnes over. They've been a big help."

"I don't suppose you'll tell me what happened?"

She shook her head. "No, and please don't ask. Just know that I will heal and be back to my old self in no time. I probably should have laid up somewhere before coming home."

"No, it's best to be with friends. If you need anything—"

"I'm fine, really. I do need to see my dad today. I'll rest a bit before I walk over."

Gunther shook his head. "No."

"No?"

"I'll carry you over in a bit. You shouldn't be walking unless you have to." His tone brooked no argument. "I've had bruised ribs and they hurt like a son of… They hurt."

"I wasn't raped. I know you think I was, but I wasn't." The doubt in his eyes was too much and biting her cheek wasn't going to work. Tears poured down her face. "Please believe me."

He touched her hand. "I do, Lee Ann. I do. I wish I could hold you, but I think I'd end up hurting you."

She took the tissues he handed her and mopped up her tears. "You're probably right. But I do thank you for the thought. It seems like a very long time went by with no one caring what happened to me."

He appeared dumbfounded. "It wasn't true you know. We all care about you here."

"I was too embarrassed to come home at first. I left here with grand ideas of making it big, but I felt defenseless against the conniving ways of others. I never learned how to insult a person while smiling. I never learned how to go behind a person's back and tell lies. I never learned how to blackmail others. I was ill equipped."

A wry smile gently curved his lips. "I'd ask you what all that meant but I'll let you be. Rest up and I'll be back in a few hours to take you to see your father." He stood and leaned over, giving her a kiss on the forehead.

All the kindness she'd received here on the ranch was like a tonic for her heart. She'd been fighting a losing battle for over a year now, and finally she didn't have to fight anymore. Would she ever feel completely safe again? She sighed. Only time would tell.

GUNTHER SAT at his desk trying his best to calm down. He rubbed his hand over his face. The phone rang and he answered it on the first ring. Upon recognizing the number on the caller ID readout, he snatched the receiver. "Any news, Andy?"

"You sitting down? Her boss Kevin Burns is a pile of dirt. No arrests, but he's been rumored to beat women, and when he wants something, he doesn't take no for an answer."

"What about rape?" Gunther held his breath.

"No. He supposedly wants his women broken and willing. He makes threats about harming their families. He's a piece of work, but no one wants to bring charges."

"How does he get away with beating women so badly they can hardly walk?" Gunther yelled.

"Hey, I'm not the enemy here, Gunther."

"I'm sorry. I have a girl who grew up on the ranch. She went to work at the magazine Burns owns." He pinched the bridge of his nose. "Somehow, he made her believe that she had no one to turn to for help. I'd like to slam my fist in his face."

"He blackballs the ones who leave him. They never work in any type of journalism job again. Andy paused, and the sound of shuffling papers came across the line. "Tell you what, get Lee Ann to give me permission to clear out her apartment for her. I'm sure it's being watched. I'll have her things shipped to you."

"Thanks." Gunther calmed a bit. "I'd appreciate that. Hey, if I can get her to testify, could we put him away?"

Andy grunted. "It's going to end up being a he said, she said situation. Those don't usually bode well for the victim. But I'll do some more digging."

Gunther sighed as he rubbed the back of his stiff neck. "I appreciate it all, Andy."

"I know you do, buddy. Keep Lee Ann safe. I don't trust Kevin Burns. I'll talk to you soon."

Gunther hung up and closed his eyes. Her boss must have scared the heck out of her. Otherwise, she wouldn't have come home. What type of man needed to beat up women and threaten them? Right now it was important that Lee Ann felt safe. Gunther had to keep her dad comfortable and keep his own anger in check. It was a tall order, but he'd get it done.

A couple hours later, he went to the foreman's house and collected Lee Ann. She was very quiet as though she had a lot on her mind.

"You hardly weigh more than a feather. Agnes will fatten you up." He carried her up the front steps.

"Most men like skinny. I was told at work I was too fat." Lee Ann's flat tone of voice concerned Gunther.

"I like all body shapes, but you could use a few pounds." He smiled into her sad eyes. "Lee Ann, you don't have to change for any man. Remember that." He carried her to her father's room and set her down on a comfortable chair. Then he took a pillow and propped it behind her. "I'll be back in a while. Good to see you, James."

"Wait! Which horse kicked her?" James asked.

"Kicked her?"

James turned his gaze to his daughter. "You were carried in here and I can see by the way you're sitting your ribs hurt. What happened?"

Her eyes widened, but she didn't say anything.

Gunther took a step forward. "It was Belle. She doesn't know Lee Ann, and you know how mares can be."

James nodded. "You okay?" He looked Lee Ann over.

Lee Ann "I'm fine. I just need a bit of rest."

"If you'll excuse me, I have a mountain of paperwork."

James waved Gunther away. "That mountain never gets any lower."

Gunther walked out of the room and headed to his office. He'd never lied to James before, and it didn't feel right but under the circumstances, it was the right thing to do. He really wanted to know every detail of what had happened to Lee Ann in San Antonio, but he'd have to let her come to him. Unfortunately, patience wasn't a virtue he possessed.

CHAPTER THREE

*I*t had been three weeks since Gunther had discovered Lee Ann's bruises. It was there in every glance; he wanted to know what had happened to her. But she had to give him credit. He didn't ask. For that, she was grateful, but she knew she'd have to tell him soon.

At least she didn't need to be carried around anymore, though she'd miss Gunther's strong arms around her. She'd been eating three meals a day, and she could see her face looked healthier. She'd been such a fool in San Antonio, and she wasn't sure how to reconcile the Lee Ann in San Antonio with the Lee Ann at the Big M Ranch. They were vastly different people, or so she thought.

She'd never be able to work for another magazine. Kevin had made sure of that. What was she to do when her father died? She couldn't pretend he was getting any better. In fact, she had a feeling it wouldn't be long now. She'd need to come up with some plan. She'd lived off Gunther's good will long enough.

Moseying on to the pasture, she glanced around. She wanted to meet Belle, the supposed kicker. Lee Ann spotted her right away. She was a beautiful, golden palomino. She tossed her head a few times as if she knew she was the prettiest one in the pasture.

A whistle from behind startled Lee Ann, and she turned around. Gunther stood a few feet away. He walked up to the white fence and Belle came right to him. He certainly had a way with the ladies.

"Some things never change," she said with a soft laugh.

"What things?"

"The females are swarming all over you."

He grinned and then shrugged. "I can't help my God-given good looks and my natural charm. Now don't be jealous, Belle. This is Lee Ann, a friend of mine. I promise not to feed her any carrots or to scratch her behind the ears. I'll save that for just you and me."

Lee Ann lightly punched Gunther in the shoulder and got the evil eye from Belle. "She seems to understand one thing. You belong to her. Have you tried putting Felicia in the pasture with Belle?" She couldn't help but smile as Gunter cocked his right brow.

"Now that might be a good idea."

"Has she decided to sell to you or is she still mad?"

He put his booted foot on the bottom rung of the fence. "She's been by a lot. I'm surprised you two didn't run into each other."

"I saw her a couple of times." Lee Ann leaned back against the fence. "I avoided her as much as possible." A sharp pain accompanied a jerk that pulled her head sideways. "Ouch!"

Gunther almost doubled over with laughter. "Belle pulled your hair with her mouth."

"What a sassy mare!" She narrowed her eyes and studied him closely. "If I remember correctly you liked sassy."

His smile faded. "I liked sassy a lot, but after you left, I wasn't in the mood. I didn't like other women being feisty to me."

She tilted her head as she gazed at him. "I missed you too. And truthfully, I wish I'd never left. My home is here, at least for a bit."

"For a bit?" He frowned.

"After Daddy is gone, I'll need to find a place. The house is rightfully Woody's. It's just the way of things. It'll be fine." She gave him a reassuring smile she in no way felt. "Well I promised Agnes I'd pick some vegetables for dinner. Her garden grows larger every year."

"Sure seems that way. I guess I should tell you. Felicia is trying to get me to marry her."

Lee Ann's jaw dropped. "What are you talking about? Tell her to take a hike."

"I wish I could. I tried being nice to her and I've tried pretending I don't want the land hoping she'd be more willing to sell. Nothing worked. I need that land. One of our main water sources comes through Old Mooney's property. Felicia has coyly mentioned she had plans to divert the water. I found out she's planning on hiring an engineer."

"Isn't that against the law?"

"I was trying to get a cease and desist order but since she just happened to mention it and didn't have any plans made my lawyer said that wasn't possible. I'd have to take her to court, and it could be a while before it's resolved. Or I can marry her and everything stays the same."

She shook her head. "No. Absolutely not. She's bluffing. She doesn't have the money to pull it off."

"I could buy a water truck and haul water up to the north pasture but the cost of it is too high." He took off his Stetson and ran his fingers through his hair then put the hat back on. "I don't know if I can take a chance that she's bluffing."

"Move the cattle to the front pasture for a while. There's

plenty of water, not as much grass though. But I bet hay would be easier to haul than water. Let her think you don't need her water."

His brow furrowed. "I hadn't thought of that. It's a great idea. When did you get to be so wise in the ways of cattle?"

"I've been the foreman's daughter all my life." She laughed. It felt so good to laugh.

"Now what do I do about Felicia?"

"That, cowboy, is your problem. Maybe your God-given talents aren't always so wonderful to have. By the way, when are my things coming? I traveled light and I didn't bring my riding boots."

"In a few days. They were packed up and shipped last night, I believe."

"I'm grateful you have a good friend in San Antonio who was able to take care of it for me. I hated to have to walk away from everything I owned, but I felt as though I didn't have a choice. Thank you."

"Don't thank me until we see if it all arrives in one piece." He grinned and tipped his hat at her. "Catch you later."

She watched him walk away. He certainly hadn't lost any of his appeal. His broad shoulders and tapered waist led to his incredibly sexy rear end. His thighs looked hard and well-muscled under his jeans. Her face grew hot. She shouldn't think like that. No man was ever going to touch her again.

Gunther had touched her a few times, of course, but out of concern. She wouldn't be able to stand it if he tried to touch her in a romantic way. She turned to Belle. "He's all yours. He told me what he thought of me when I left two years ago. He believed me to be a snob because I wanted a different life. I just didn't want to wait around to see who he married and had babies with." She chuckled. Talking to Belle was better than talking to herself.

GUNTHER SAT at his desk wondering which vegetables they'd be having for dinner. The subject had never really interested him before. He was jarred from his musing by a knock on the door.

"Come in."

Agnes opened the door and walked to his desk. She handed him a manila envelope. "This just came for you. Looks important."

He took the envelope and nodded. "Thanks." He opened it while Agnes left closing the door behind her.

He furrowed his brow when he saw the return address had Kevin Burns' name on it. What could Lee Ann's old boss need to send to him? He opened it, pulled out a photo and was immediately enraged. Lee Ann didn't have any clothes on. He closed his eyes and fumed. Then it occurred to him he'd seen a window in the picture.

Opening his eyes again, he studied the photograph while trying not to focus on Lee Ann. It had been taken from outside her window. Her clothes were on the bed and she had a towel in her hand. Some slime ball took these pictures without her consent. Damn, what else had happened at that job?

To tell Lee Ann or not? He groaned. It would be better to tell her, but he didn't want to see her reaction. Why did she have to go and leave the ranch two years back? He certainly understood the need to spread her wings, but she had grown up too sheltered. All potential love interests from his cowboys had been warned off by him. Looking back, Gunther realized he'd just been selfish. He wanted her for himself, and when she'd left he had felt hurt and betrayed.

He picked up the phone and called Detective Morellis. "Andy, we have a problem."

"Hey, Gunther. I was just about to call you. I went to her apartment and someone had gotten to it before me."

"Her stuff is gone?"

"No. In fact, you'll get it day after tomorrow. Someone went in and planted things to make it seem as though she was a highly sexual woman with strange desires."

Gunther took a deep breath and let it out slowly. "What do you mean?"

"Sexy lingerie and a few toys here and there. Magazines too. But it was all brand new, never worn, used, or even looked at. They stupidly left price tags on most of it. I'm not quite sure of the why yet."

"I received a naked picture of Lee Ann in the mail. It was taken from outside her window. She was obviously heading to take a shower. Why would Kevin Burns go to so much trouble? I can't figure out his game."

Andy sighed. "My guess is that he expects you to throw her off your property, and he'll be waiting for her. I asked around. He blackmailed many women where he works. First, he promises better jobs while he beats them. I'm guessing the pictures are to keep them from going to the police. He threatens their families if they leave. He threatens their careers too. Eventually, he gets tired of them and lets them go, but they never find jobs writing again. No one will testify, and they only talked off the record."

"My God! Did he have sex with these women?" Gunther held his breath.

"Many, yes, but from what I've gathered, not Lee Ann. At least that is the rumor."

Gunther let out his breath and ran his hand over his face. "She's in danger."

"I think so. Play it safe and smart. Do you want me to call your local police department?"

"No, let me talk to Lee Ann first. Andy, thank you."

"Anytime. Listen, if I find out anything else I'll be in touch. Be careful."

"Will do." Gunther hung up the phone and leaned back in his leather chair. How did men like Burns get away with using his power to control women? Shaking his head, he realized he already knew the answer. People still didn't believe a woman who spoke out about bad treatment, especially since Burns finally got them to agree to sleep with him. Gunther wanted to wrap his hands around Kevin Burns' neck and squeeze.

He looked up at the ceiling. He wasn't a violent man, but this whole situation had made him madder than he'd ever been. Now, how to tell Lee Ann about the picture.

CHAPTER FOUR

*T*he moon illuminated the sky, and the stars twinkled brightly. It was a beautiful sight to behold. Lee Ann smiled, and her worries felt lighter as she walked with Gunther to the gazebo. The torchlights were lit and a coffee pot and mugs sat waiting on the table.

"It's lovely out here," said Lee Ann, surprised at the cheerfulness in her voice.

"It sure is. I didn't sit out here the whole time you were gone. It would have felt too lonely."

Turning her head, she stared at him. "I don't remember us parting on such good terms."

Gunther took her hand, led her up the steps to the gazebo, and pulled out her chair for her.

She sat and poured their coffee then waited until he was seated. "What did you want to talk about? I want you to know I've sent out my resume and made calls, but no one is hiring right now." She clenched her hands into fists. "The truth is no one is hiring *me* right now. My old boss's reach was much longer than I ever thought."

"I'm not here to talk about you getting a job." He looked troubled.

"What's wrong?" Her heart dropped.

He hesitated, and a muscle worked in his jaw. "I received mail from your old boss today."

Her heart pounded and her stomach clenched. This was it. He was going to ask her to leave. "What was it?"

"It was a picture of you…"

Tears pricked at the back of her eyes as shame washed over her. "He said he had pictures. I never posed for them, I swear!"

Gunther reached across the table and took her small hand in his big hand. "It was taken from outside your window."

"Did I have clothes on?" Her body began to shake as she waited for his answer.

"No, no you didn't." His voice was so gentle it touched her soul.

She shifted her gaze to the ground. She couldn't look at him anymore. "My apartment was backed up against a beautiful, heavily treed forest. I didn't think to close the blinds all the time. I figured no one could see me. I'm such a fool. This is all my fault. I'm too stupid to even close my blinds." She felt ill. Gunther had now seen her naked.

She gathered her courage and glanced up at him. "When do you want me out of here?"

"Honey, I'm not asking you to leave. Not now, not ever. This is your home, no matter what happens. Okay? You need to feel secure and safe, and I'm hoping the Big M Ranch can do that for you. I hope me and Agnes, Woody, and all the men can do that."

Swallowing hard she nodded. "Thank you. I do feel as though this is my home but the house—"

"Woody has a high-end trailer that he happens to love. I asked him if he wanted the house. You're right, he should live there, but he doesn't want it. You need to go and look at his place. I'm paying him too much. He has a huge big screen television, state of the art surround sound. Everything in it is top of the line, even the refrigerator. He implied that the house would take too much work to fix up."

"Leave it to Woody to have a good reason not to take a house. But I'm glad. One less worry. "I can't pay rent until I find a job, but I do want to earn my keep around here."

His heart-stopping grin always made her smile. He had the cutest dimple in his cheek, which he always denied was there. "If I remember correctly you're a hell of a horse trainer. I have some three-year-olds ready to be trained. Angus was just grumbling the other day about me breeding more horses than he had time for."

A giggle slipped out. "I like Angus, a bit gruff but he has a big heart. He taught me how to ride and train horses."

Gunther laughed. "I know, I was there, remember?"

She nodded and then grew serious. "How many pictures do you think Kevin Burns has of me? The thought makes me sick to my stomach. I can't believe he sent one to you. I bet he expected you to throw me out so I'd go crawling back to him."

"I didn't stare at the picture. I just looked at the details of where it was taken and so forth. I put it in the safe so no one else will see it."

She nodded. Even if he didn't stare at it, he'd *seen* it. Humiliation filled her whole being. Gunther would never think of her as a good, innocent woman again. He'd think of her as tainted. He'd had girlfriends she was pretty sure he'd slept with, and there was nothing wrong with that, but she had grown up believing people should wait until they were married. Now, he probably thought her easy, though he'd never say it.

"Thank you for locking it up. I should have figured Kevin

would know where I was. I'm so tired, Gunther. I think I'll turn in."

He nodded and stood. "I'll walk you home."

She shook her head as she stood up. "If you don't mind I'd rather walk alone. I have some thinking to do. This is a lot to take in."

He put his arm around her shoulders and kissed her cheek. "Get some rest. I don't want you spending too much time with the horses. I'd rather you were with your dad."

"Thanks. Me too." She walked around the main house and to the foreman's house. Only it wasn't the foreman's house anymore, she mused. She sat on the top step in front of the house and laid her forehead on her knees. *I am strong, I am courageous, I can do this*, she chanted in her head. She just wished she believed that.

A WEEK LATER, Gunther stood in front of the mirror in his bedroom tying his tie. It was hard to believe James was gone. It had been expected, but still nothing could prepare a person for a love one's death. Sadness permeated the whole ranch. But what worried Gunther the most was the lack of tears from Lee Ann. She had been with him when he died, and she'd calmly found Gunther and told him.

As soon as he heard, he'd sprinted to James' room and cried like a baby, but not Lee Ann. She just stood and stared. He wanted to comfort her, but she didn't invite comforting not even from Agnes. Maybe she was in denial? Hell, he didn't know anything about women. But he did know Lee Ann. They'd grown up together, and while she had grit, she also had a sensitive and compassionate heart.

One time they'd been playing in the woods with their sling shots and he had killed a rabbit. He'd jumped up and down, so excited, but Lee Ann had given him a look of disgust before she ran away from him. She hadn't talked to him for three days. He'd finally picked her some flowers, and Agnes made snickerdoodles for him to give Lee Ann. She had forgiven him, but he had known it was only because those were her favorite cookies.

Too bad cookies wouldn't help now. Being an adult wasn't all it was cracked up to be. He didn't know all the answers or any of them for that matter. He wasn't old enough or wise enough. Sure, he could run the ranch with his eyes closed, but he'd been trained from birth.

He put on his black suit jacket and squared his shoulders. They carried a lot of weight. The first step was to get through the funeral, then the wake. He'd been to many funerals in his life that he'd lost count, but for some reason this was the hardest one. In some ways, he felt broken but he'd pretend he wasn't.

He went down the stairs, and Agnes stood there waiting. She wore the same black dress she always wore to funerals. She immediately adjusted his tie and then smiled at him. "He'll be greatly missed. I hired a caterer for afterward."

"Good. Thank you. I don't know what I'd do without you, Agnes."

"You won't need to find out. I plan on living forever. The limo is here to take us. Why don't you go and get Lee Ann." She practically pushed him out of the door.

He nodded to Woody and Shelly, who were already out front waiting near the limo and then walked across the yard to Lee Ann's house. He didn't even have to knock on the door. She opened it as he walked up the steps. She wore a beautiful burgundy dress and she looked pretty as a picture except for the pain in her eyes.

"I'm ready," she said, clutching her purse in both hands.

He held out his arm, and she took it. The walk to the limo

was slow and silent, but finally he got her settled in. The rest joined them, the mood somber as they drove. No one said a word. Lee Ann looked out the window the whole time.

The graveside was crowded, but the seats were empty. Gunther escorted Lee Ann to a wooden folding chair and sat next to her. She had such a grip on her purse, her knuckles had turned white. They went through the motions of a graveside service, though Gunther didn't hear a single word the minister intoned, and Lee Ann still hadn't uttered a word. After the service, she only nodded at people who offered condolences.

It was a relief to get back to the ranch. Gunther took off his tie first thing. He greeted people and directed them to the bar and the food. A feeling of being watched came over him, and he glanced up. The instant he spotted Felicia, he groaned out loud.

She made a beeline for him. "Such a tragedy," she said as she took both of his hands. "Is there anything I can do?"

"Thank you, but no." Lee Ann's voice startled him. He could have sworn she'd been sitting on the couch.

Felicia stared at her for a moment. "Burgundy, what an interesting choice of color for a funeral."

"Thank you," Lee Ann clipped.

"I mean, aren't you supposed to wear black? Perhaps you couldn't afford a new dress? I heard you got fired from your last job."

Gunther pulled his hands away from her. "Felicia—"

"This is the last dress my father saw me in, and he had remarked how beautiful I looked in it. I wore it in his honor, not to please you." Lee Ann turned on her heel and headed toward the bar.

Felicia put her hand to her mouth. "Oh my I didn't mean—"

Gunther gave her a look of disgust. "Yes, you did." He

turned and walked away. He wasn't in the mood for Felicia and her games. He panned the room and saw Lee Ann talking to Angus. Good, maybe she could keep her mind off things.

He grabbed a scotch from the bar and headed over to them.

"It was taped to Belle's stall. I really didn't mean to tell you today. I'm sorry." Angus looked upset.

Lee Ann took Gunther's scotch and finished it in one shot. "I'm glad you told me, Angus. I need to know what's going on."

Gunther looked from one to the other. "What?"

"It's all right, Angus. I'll tell Gunther. By the way, where is the picture now?"

"I burned it up. I'll let you talk." Angus gave him a look of apology before he walked away.

"Let's go outside to talk," he suggested and was relieved when she nodded.

Taking her hand, he slowly led her through the crowd and outside. "On second thought, it's too crowded out here too. Let's walk down to the stream."

"That would be best," she said woodenly.

They walked through a wooded area for a bit and found the bench they had made when they were kids. Lee Ann smiled when she saw it.

"I'm glad I didn't wear high heels today."

"I bet it made for easier walking." They sat side by side. "The bench is smaller than I remember."

She smiled again. "We used to be smaller." Her smile faded. "Do you think Kevin was here at the ranch? I'm so embarrassed that Angus saw a nude photo of me. I don't know what I'm supposed to do, and I have no one to ask. My dad…" She trailed off and was silent as she just stared at the stream.

"I haven't seen you cry."

"And you won't. If I start, I'll end up a weeping mess. It's a sad day, but my anger is taking over. Do you think he put more pictures around the ranch? What if more than just Angus saw the picture? Gunther, I need to leave this place. I need to find a place to hide." She pressed both palms against her temples. "How could someone do such a thing? First, they invade my privacy and take pictures of me, and then they compound the injury by showing the pictures. This must be against the law. I feel so violated. I should have just let him use me as a punching bag. At least I could hide it. He never touched my face. My whole life is ruined."

"Hey, only Angus and I saw the pictures, and we saw them for what they are." He softened his tone and stroked her arm just above her wrist. "We didn't take any delight in seeing you without clothes on. You're not the type of girl who would allow anyone to take pictures of you that way. I'll see if anyone wants extra pay for guard duty. I can get outside help if needed. I wish this was enough to put Kevin in jail but it's not. I hate that you have to go through this."

"It seems as though the law is on his side." She sounded miserable, like she was giving up.

He nodded. "It sure does seem that way. He's done this to countless girls, but there isn't any evidence. I think you're the only one who actually defied him and left. That's probably why he's been sending the photos."

Lee Ann put her hands over her face. "Now he's trying to ruin my life. I just buried my father! I want to scream and cry and hurt Kevin, but I just can't. You don't think he's going to stop do you?"

"We'll make reports with the police. Maybe with enough incidents we can get him on stalking. I don't know the law. We'll have to see."

She clasped her hands on her lap as she stared at the water again. "Do you remember our first kiss?"

He grunted. "Yes, and all the hell I got."

She gave him a smile. "I kissed you and you told your dad because you were mad. Then you told my dad and everyone laughed at your outrage."

"You had cooties and having them all laugh only made it worse." He shot her a grin. "Like I said you were always so sassy."

"You wouldn't let me follow you for a whole month. It was the loneliest time of my life. My dad thought learning to do house work would keep me busy. I cursed you with every dish I washed and vowed never to kiss you again."

He couldn't help but stare at her plump lips. They looked luscious but she wouldn't want to know that. "Sometimes things change. I once vowed never to take another bath as long as I lived but that vow only lasted until my father dumped me in the tub with my clothes on."

Her laughter lightened his heart. She was just so beautiful, and he wanted to kiss her. He wanted his lips touching hers, but he decided it would be too much for her to handle. Besides, they were best friends, and he couldn't ruin that for her. He needed her too.

"I'll see about setting up more security. We really should get back."

"Yes, Felicia is probably looking for you," she joked.

"Yes, I like a woman who insults others and tries to blackmail me into marrying her." He chuckled. "Let's go."

LEE ANN HELPED Agnes clean up after the caterers left. They did a decent job, but Agnes was fussy about her kitchen. It didn't take long, and Lee Ann snuck off to her house without saying good bye. She wasn't up for any more heartfelt words. People meant well, and her father had been well-loved, but she needed to decompress. Plus she hated wearing pantyhose.

Jeans, T-shirts, boots, and a Stetson was the outfit she liked best. She wasn't sure what she had thought when she left the ranch. Maybe she'd thought she was above living the simple life. She'd wanted to experience life in a city and make the people she loved see that she was much more than wife and mother material. She wasn't one to allow another to make decisions for her and from what she could see, that was what marriage meant. A wife obeyed her husband. Well, she was her own person, and she had set out to prove it.

Sighing, she sat on the bed. She had proved something all right. That she was too young and stupid. She was exactly what everyone thought she was. A foolish, naive girl who'd come back with her tail between her legs. Restless, she stood and walked to the window. No one actually said it, but it was how she felt.

She toyed with the edge of the curtain. Why hadn't she made more time for her daddy? She should have called more, and she should have come home to visit. At least she'd had a bit of time with him. His spirit had been so calm and serene on his last day. He knew death was knocking at his door and he accepted it. In the days before he died, their souls were both calm with no worries. They each knew that the other would be just fine. They didn't even have to talk much, it was as though they could see inside each other's hearts and that was how they'd said good-bye. Hopefully she made his passing easier.

Tears welled up in her eyes and poured down her face. She grabbed his pillow off the bed, held it, and smelled it. It still had his scent on it. The hole in her heart would probably always be there. Her grief grew stronger as she hugged his pillow to her. He had left her one gift. The gift of being self-sufficient. It was the type of gift that mattered. She cried herself to sleep.

THE NEXT MORNING she was ready to start training the horses. Horses were easier to work with than most people she knew. They each had their own personalities and quirks. Some were friendly and others a bit standoffish. Some were gentle while others would just as soon kick a person. But that was what the training was for. Mostly, she wanted to see Sabrina, her rescue horse. She'd seen her in the pasture, but with everything going on she hadn't had time to love on her.

Sabrina had been starved and had to be hoisted out of the horse buy lot, some called it the kill pens. Gunther had thought her crazy and said she'd only get her heart broken when the horse died. For the first few days, the poor mare just stood in one place in her stall, shaking. But slowly over time, they'd created a bond. She wasn't the smartest horse, probably from malnutrition; her brain hadn't received all the vital nutrients it had needed.

But that didn't matter. She was sweet as could be, and all Lee Ann wanted was for Sabrina to be happy. There were no plans to ride her. She was small for her age, and she might not understand what was going on with a saddle. It was better that she just do what she was doing, learning how to be a horse.

Whistling as she walked into the barn, Lee Ann was happy when Sabrina cried out to her. That greeting was a balm to her soul. Lee Ann immediately grabbed a brush and went into Sabrina's stall.

"Hey, girl. Long time. How have you been?" She took the brush and began to groom the mare. "You look beautiful. Don't tell the other mares but you're the prettiest one here.

Your beauty can be seen in your eyes, you have a sweet heart. I'll be around for a while, so we'll see a lot of each other." She patted Sabrina's neck and let herself out of the stall.

"I'm glad to hear you plan to stay." Gunther stood leaning against the outside of the stall.

"I'm taking your job offer. I wanted to say hello to Sabrina before I assess the three-year-olds."

"I'm going to ride up toward Felicia's to see if she started diverting the water yet."

"Did you want me to saddle your horse?"

He laughed. "The day I can't saddle my own horse is the day I'm too old to be riding. Thanks for the offer but you're not the stable boy."

"I know. I was just being nice."

Gunther got his paint ready to go. "You can just be yourself."

She blinked at him. "Does that mean that I'm not usually nice?"

He stepped forward and cupped her chin gently in his hand. He turned her face and kissed her cheek before he let go. "No that wasn't what I meant. I'll see you in a few hours."

She watched him lead his horse out of the barn then they were off. Gunther always had a good seat. Her face heated. His jeans looked real nice on him too.

A few hours later, she was heading back to the house. She needed a shower. It felt as though all of the Texas dust was on her.

"Lee Ann! There's a phone call for you!" Agnes yelled from the front porch of the main house.

Stopping in her tracks, her heart skipped a beat. Her hands became fisted by her sides. "Did they say who's calling?"

"No, but he said it was very important."

"Thanks." Lee Ann changed direction and walked into the main house.

"You can take it in Gunther's office."

She nodded to Agnes as she walked down the hall and into the large office. A part of her wanted to ignore the call and just hang up the phone. But that wouldn't solve anything. She hesitantly picked up the phone. "Hello?"

"So good to hear your voice again."

A chill went up her spine, and her stomach turned sour at Kevin's words. "Not really. I'd rather not talk to you."

"I don't like unfinished business, Lee Ann," Kevin said.

"Nothing's unfinished. I've moved on, and I suggest you do the same." She clutched the edge of the desk to steady herself. "There must be some other woman you're manhandling already. If I had proof you'd be in jail."

"Lee Ann..." He clicked his tongue. "You don't understand. We're not done unless I say we're done."

"Go to hell!" She slammed down the phone and dropped down onto Gunther's leather chair. Her heart pumped so fast it hurt. What had Kevin meant, they weren't done? Wrapping her arms around herself, she realized nowhere was safe. But really what more could he do that he hadn't done already?

CHAPTER FIVE

A week later Gunther received a call from Woody telling him they needed to talk in person. Woody wouldn't tell him what the problem was over the phone, and the summons left Gunther wondering. Felicia must be up to something. He tried to concentrate on his paperwork while he waited but gave up and sat rubbing the back of his tense neck.

Woody knocked and walked in. His expression was one of fury. "I have to show you something."

Gunther started to stand but Woody gestured for him to stay where he was. Then Woody walked behind the desk and angled the keypad his way. "You're not going to like this." He typed in an internet address and up came pictures of Lee Ann. Many pictures, disgusting pictures.

Gunther felt as though he couldn't breathe for a moment. "Can we get this taken down?"

Woody shook his head. "I think it's time to call the police. I don't know the first thing about taking sites down."

Frowning, Gunther raised his brow as he looked at Woody. "How did you find the site?"

Woody went back in front of the desk and sat down. "It was in my email."

With a growl, Gunther slapped the top of his desk. "I wonder who else got the email."

Woody glanced away. "Everyone on the ranch as far as I know. But the internet reaches millions of people so I couldn't even begin to guess." He looked back at Gunther. I wanted you to know before Lee Ann got wind of it."

"Too late." Lee Ann stood in the doorway looking as white as a sheet. "I should have known the phone call wasn't the end of it. Gunther, what am I going to do? Everyone has probably seen the pictures by now. They were in my email too."

"Come in," Gunther said as he stood. The way she ran into his embrace surprised him. He wrapped his arms around her and rocked her back and forth.

"Woody, could you call the police for me?"

Woody stood. "I'd be happy to. Lee Ann, I'm sorry this is happening to you."

Her face was buried in Gunther's chest. "Thank you," she mumbled. She tightened her hold.

He stroked her back, not knowing what else to do. He didn't take to feeling helpless well. He was always the one everyone looked to for the answers.

"I'm so sorry, sweetheart." When she came up for air, he led her to a chair and helped her sit. "What's this about a phone call?" He handed her a tissue.

She wiped away her tears and sat up straight and tall. "Kevin called and said we have unfinished business. I told him to go to hell."

Gunther sat down in the chair next to her and took her hand. It seemed so small and fragile but he knew she was much stronger than she looked. "Good for you, honey. He was bound to do this regardless of what you said to him. I hope we can put him in jail."

"He seems to think he's untouchable."

He gave her hand a squeeze. "We'll have to wait to see what the police say."

THE MORE DETECTIVE Billings talked the more anxious Lee Ann became. He was going to get the cybercrime unit involved, but he doubted there was anything they could do. "We really don't have enough here to call it stalking."

"That's not true," Lee Ann said. "I looked it up for Texas. It's stalking if the perpetrator makes the victim feel harassed, annoyed, alarmed, abused, tormented, embarrassed, or offended."

"That is part of the statute but I won't be able to get an arrest warrant for this. How do we know you didn't approve of the pictures being taken? You were in a relationship with this Kevin Burns."

"They were clearly taken from outside my window. How could I approve that?"

The detective shifted in the chair. "I know this is upsetting, and I'd be just as outraged as you. The cyber unit may be able to find the site and have it taken down, but I have to warn you they usually pop right back up."

She nodded. He just didn't get it. Then again, how could he? He probably wouldn't care if naked pictures of him were all over the internet. "What do I do if he calls again?"

"I suggest letting all numbers you don't recognize go straight to voice message. Otherwise, just hang up. You might want to block his number."

Gunther stood and walked around to the front of his desk. "Thank you for taking the time to come out here,

Detective Billings. We appreciate your advice. Let me walk you out."

As soon as they left she sat at the desk and began a Google search of Kevin Burns. Bile rose as she saw one article after another featuring him as a wonderfully innovative publisher of a chic magazine. There wasn't a bad word about him anywhere. How could that be true? There must be something unflattering about him on the internet. It looked as though he had the whole world fooled.

"What are you up to?" Gunther asked as he came back into the office and sat in a chair.

"I was looking to see if I could find any dirt on Kevin, but so far I'm coming up with nothing but praise for the golden boy. It makes me sick." She stopped to take a calming breath. "I'll never be able to show my face in public again. And no, I'm not being dramatic."

"I never said you were. I wish I had some wonderful words of wisdom for you, but I really don't know what to say." He balled his fists. "I really want to choke the breath out of him, but that for sure is a punishable crime."

"Thank you for wanting to defend my honor, but I think I don't have any honor left." A sad smile tugged at her lips. "I'm just glad my dad isn't here to see all this. It's crazy that they can't make him take down the pictures of me. It is the most humiliating thing that people I know have seen these photos. I tried to walk the straight and narrow like Daddy taught me, and this is what I got. I'm so stupid. I should have quit the first time he hit me.'" She released a heavy sigh. "It's my own greedy fault. I really wanted to write for the magazine instead of always getting coffee for everyone. He invited me to dinner, and the next day I got to do that stupid poll about bathing suits. It wasn't much, but I was so thrilled and proud of my accomplishment."

He scrubbed his face with his hand and shook his head.

"Come, let's get some fresh air." He touched her shoulder and she flinched away. Even though he'd seen the naked pictures of her before, something about knowing he was no longer the only person who'd seen them made her feel too dirty to enjoy even the simplest gesture.

"How could I have let this happen? I can't go outside. They've seen me." Her body began to tremble, and she couldn't seem to stop it.

Gunther knelt down and took her hand. "Take a deep breath and let it out slowly." He waited until she was done. "Now again." He nodded. "How about we ride out to check on the cattle?"

She shook her head and glanced away from him. "I don't feel like horseback riding." Her chin quivered, and she waited for the dreaded tears to start but they didn't.

"We can just sit and relax here then," Gunther said in a soft voice.

"I'm going to go to my house. I need time alone." A lump formed in her throat. She was grateful he didn't say anything that he just let her go.

When she reached her house, she walked in and sighed in relief. She closed the door and leaned her back against it then slowly slid down to the floor. She pulled her knees up so she could lay her head against them and cried. This whole thing was like a bullet in her heart, and she wasn't sure how much more she could take.

Everyone had to be laughing at her. She was just a country hick who had been ripe for the picking. She'd never had a boyfriend. Well, there was Gunther and at one time, she'd thought... But then he'd started dating, and she couldn't stay and watch. She'd loved him since forever, but he only saw her as a playmate he'd had when he was a kid. Why he had been so mad when she left, she never could figure out.

After high school, she had written for the local newspaper, and that had given her the confidence to apply for the magazine job. When she landed that job, she was beyond joyful until she had run and told Gunther. He gazed at her as if he didn't even know her. He scowled and told her she wasn't meant for big city life. He had drained her joy, and she'd never felt joy like that since.

His attitude had made her glad to leave. Any illusions she'd had about a "someday" with him had died, though, she had thought of him often while she was away. He was a good man, a kind man, a strong man and a very, very handsome man. It wasn't his fault he hadn't wanted her the way she'd wanted him.

He still didn't, and she'd learn to accept it. He was friendly but he hadn't made a move toward her. His help was what she needed the most.

CHAPTER SIX

*T*wo weeks later, Gunter sat at the kitchen table drumming his fingers. His jaw was clenched as he shook his head. How was he going to get Lee Ann to leave the foreman's house? She refused to step outside. Every time he mentioned it, she had a near panic attack, and he was out of ideas.

She'd lost weight and often gave him a blank stare. Nothing new had happened, thankfully. Andy Morellis had found more victims in San Antonio. Still, no one would testify. Maybe he should take Lee Ann down there to talk to a few of these women, not to get them to testify but so she'd know she wasn't alone.

He sighed. It wouldn't work. He'd have to kidnap her to get her to go. Those years she'd been away, he'd missed her more than he ever wanted to admit. He was glad she was home but not under these circumstances. He'd spent those years wanting her to come home—to him. She never had. Now it was too late. She shied away if he touched her. At first, she allowed an occasional kiss on the cheek, but now it was hands off.

"Boss come quick and grab your gun!" Woody was breathing hard as he talked. "That Kevin guy is pounding on Lee Ann's door."

Quick as he could manage, Gunther grabbed his gun and ran out the back door, rounded the back of Lee Ann's house and slowly moved toward the front. He got to the corner and said a quick prayer.

"Burns you're not welcome here!" he yelled out. His heart pounded painfully against his chest.

"I'm just here to get what's owed to me," Kevin shot back.

Gunther peeked around the corner. Kevin's face was mottled red but his hands were empty; he didn't appear to have a gun. Gunther took a step beyond the corner. "This is private property. As of right now you're trespassing."

Kevin narrowed his eyes and his lips formed a thin line. "Very well, I'd be happy to leave. Could you tell Lee Ann I stopped by? I just wanted to catch up." He walked down the steps and without even glancing in Gunther's way, he got into his car and drove away.

As soon as the car was out of sight, Lee Ann came out with a bag. "I'm staying at the main house." She hurried by Gunther and made a mad dash for the house, reminding him of a scared rabbit.

He shook his head. He'd expected tears or maybe that she'd slump against him so he could pick her up and carry her. Instead, she'd packed a bag and made a run for the house. He couldn't help the grin that crossed his face. She never failed to surprise him.

Maybe the tears would come when he got to the house.

Lee Ann stood by the door with her hands on her hips. He closed the door behind him and stared at her.

"Just who does he think he is? I want a gun! How dare he come here? I knew he was crazy but— Hey, can we call the police and see if *this* is stalking?" She started to pace. "He'll be back, you know. That's why I'm moving in. I don't trust him. Which bedroom should I take? I think the one next to yours would be best."

"Whoa, honey." He stepped farther into the room. "Slow down a bit. He's gone for now, and we can take one question at a time."

She simply nodded, grabbed her bag, and quickly went up the stairs. So much for deciding the answers together. She seemed to have it all under control.

LEE ANN CLOSED the bedroom door and leaned against it with her arms wrapped around her waist to keep her from going to pieces. Kevin just wanted to prove he could get to her anywhere. The thought of him made her stomach roil. He told her she'd regret it if she left and he was right.

She shook her head. No, she didn't regret leaving, just hated what he was doing now. She'd been one step away from buying a gun. She knew how to shoot, but she was afraid she'd end up in jail for killing Kevin. She'd threatened to go the board of directors until Kevin pointed out a few her female coworkers who he said were sleeping with men on the board.

There had been nowhere to turn and Kevin took delight in her predicament. He'd called her a high-class whore. She walked to the window and laughed. A virgin whore. How ridiculous was that?

The knock she knew was coming brought her from her musings. "Come in." She wasn't one bit surprised to see Gunther.

"You did say the room next to mine?" He smiled at her.

"Yes, is that okay?" Every way she turned, she ended up doing something wrong.

"After my dad died, I moved into the master bedroom." He held out his hand.

She grabbed her bag and then his hand and then allowed him to lead her down the hallway.

Gunther opened a door. "You'll be more comfortable here."

Lee Ann frowned. "This is your old room." She looked around and noticed all new furniture. "Looks much better than when you had it."

"I wanted a guest room. I have cattle buyers who come here for meetings, and some have to travel a long way. In fact, you picked the only room that hasn't been redone."

"Did you update the bathroom too?"

"Yes, no more running outside to the outhouse." He laughed.

She gave him a light punch in his arm. "You know that's not what I meant. The old faucet always dripped, and the floor was warped."

"All updated. I've had a few good years and debated whether or not to bulldoze the place and start over, but this house has too much history. I left downstairs pretty much the same with new appliances and bathroom. Agnes picked out the furniture."

He made her feel lighthearted. "I thought decorating with duct tape was in vogue."

His dimples showed as his grin widened. "It got to be too difficult with all the new colors and patterns. I couldn't decide."

"I remember years when we weren't sure we'd all have a roof over our heads. Your dad and mine used to whisper about it all the time. At one point, I thought your father was going to sell."

He sat in a plush chair near the window. "That was before oil was found on the property. My dad signed a contract which only gave him twenty percent of the take. It was more money than we ever thought but he felt cheated. He swore no more drilling on his land."

Lee Ann joined him at the window. "You made it prosper. In fact, you've made everyone happy. Agnes is in heaven with the bigger garden. Angus loves the horses, and I'm happy you gave me a job. I'm just sorry about the trouble I brought with me." She released a wistful sigh.

Gunther slowly put his arms around her and set her on his lap. He tucked her head under his chin. "That trouble is not of your making. I still can't understand how it isn't illegal to post pictures on the internet."

"He's just covering his actions. It makes me look like a willing participant to his perversions. I just hate that all the hands saw the pictures of me."

"If anyone gets out of line, you let me know immediately. I'll do my best to keep you safe."

A few hours later, Lee Ann could still feel the special warmth that only Gunther could provide. He was a good man. Why hadn't he been scooped up by some woman? He was quite the catch.

She went downstairs to help Agnes with dinner. There really wasn't much left to do. There was a chicken in the oven along with vegetables. Fresh bread was already on the counter cooling along with a peach pie.

"It smells so good in here. Agnes, you are a wonder!"

Agnes smiled. "I've had years of practice. It's easy once you get the hang of it. If I remember correctly you're a good cook yourself."

"I never remember my kitchen smelling as good as this, though. Agnes, why do you think Gunther never married?"

Agnes shook her head. "I don't get into his business."

Lee Ann wanted to laugh. Agnes knew what Gunther was up to before he did. "I understand."

"Understand what?" Lee Ann jumped at the sound of Gunther's voice.

"Why you never married," Lee Ann said. She crossed her arms across her chest as she stared at him.

"I've been busy. Of course, I've dated, but nothing stuck." He cocked one brow at Lee Ann. "Was there anything else you wanted to know?"

Her face heated and she wanted to squirm under his stare. "No, I think that covers it." She quickly turned her back to him and began to slice the bread.

"Speaking of girlfriends, Felicia is coming to dinner," Agnes announced. "She said she was invited."

Lee Ann glanced over her shoulder at Gunther. His brow furrowed as he frowned.

"I didn't invite her. I guess we'll find out when she gets here. She still refuses to sell that piece of land to me. Dang, I wish I were married, then she wouldn't be looking for me to marry her."

Agnes took Lee Ann's hand and then grabbed Gunther's until they stood side by side. "I now pronounce you two engaged. Let's see if that gets her panties in a knot." She smiled at the couple. "Wait right here!" She hurried off.

Lee Ann didn't know where to look so she stared at the floor. It was one thing after another.

"Here it is! Gunther this was your mother's engagement ring. It's a bit modest but I think history trumps carats." She handed the ring to Gunther and then put her hands on her hips. "Well?"

Gunther stared at the ring. "I remember my mother wearing it. My dad offered to get her a bigger diamond but she wouldn't hear of it." He turned toward Lee Ann. "What do you think? It just might work."

She closed her eyes for a moment. She'd often dreamed of this happening but not in a false way. She swallowed hard.

Marriage was something she took seriously. But she wanted to help Gunther. Nodding her head, she held her hand out. The ring fit perfectly.

"I'll try not to lose it," she teased.

"Oh my, Gunther get a bottle of champagne out so we can celebrate at dinner. I'll get the crystal champagne flutes. This is going to be so much fun." Agnes hurried out of the kitchen.

Lee Ann stared at the ring. It was beautiful, and Gunther's mother was right; the sentiment was worth much more than a bigger diamond. If only Gunther had given it to her out of love.

She smiled. On the other hand, seeing Felicia's face might be fun.

GUNTHER FIXED HIS TIE, wondering if they were going too far. Felicia could refuse to sell out of spite. He took his tie back off. They couldn't go through with it. It was just wrong. That was not the way he wanted to propose to Lee Ann. Shocked, he looked at himself in his bedroom mirror. Why such a thought popped into his head, he had no idea.

Someone was going to end up hurt. He walked out of his room, planning to put an end to the farce. Felicia's voice coming from the living room grated on his nerves, and he cringed. There was no backing out now. It was going to be pure misery touching Lee Ann, knowing she hated to be touched.

As soon as one foot hit the first floor, Felicia was upon him.

"Engaged? What a surprise, Gunther. Somehow I'm finding it hard to believe." Her eyes flashed with rage.

"Not so hard, I'm sure." He walked over to the chair Lee Ann sat on and kissed her cheek. "We grew up together."

Lee Ann glanced up at him and gave him a loving smile. Hoo boy, she was a good actress.

"Is that so?" Felicia sat down in the chair next to Lee Ann. She sat at the edge of the seat.

Lee Ann nodded. "One of the reasons I left the ranch in the first place was because Gunther saw me as a child and not as the woman I was. I was wearing my heart out on him, and just became too hard."

"As far as I could tell by looking at pictures on the internet, you bounced back rather quickly. Wouldn't you agree, Gunther?"

He seethed while trying to maintain an outward look of calm. "We're putting that unfortunate happening behind us. I know we have a bright and happy future ahead of us." He brushed a strand of hair out of her eyes. "Don't we, darling?"

Lee Ann nodded. "I'm very blessed. Shall we take our seats in the dining room?" She stood, put her arm through his, and glanced up at him with a warm smile.

Gunther gestured for Felicia to go ahead of them. He glanced at Lee Ann and winked at her. Her blush warmed him.

Agnes stood next to the table with a bottle of champagne in her hand. "Gunther, would you open this? I never did get the hang of it."

Gunther kissed Agnes on her cheek as he took the bottle from her. "Grab a glass for yourself. You've been a big part of our lives."

Happiness spread over her face as she took a crystal flute from the cabinet. It seemed so right, Gunther had to remind himself it was all pretend. He filled each glass and then raised his to Lee Ann.

"I've known you forever. You know what I'm going to say before I even say it. It broke my heart the day you left, and I'm so glad you're back. Thank you for saying yes when I asked you to marry me." He took a sip of his champagne as did the others. All he wanted to do was lean over and kiss Lee Ann, but he didn't want to overplay his hand.

Felicia wasn't enjoying herself if the hangdog expression on her face was any indication.

"Congrats. Too bad your dad wasn't here to walk you down the aisle." She seated herself at the table.

Gunther groaned inwardly. Happiness seemed to drain out of Lee Ann. Felicia definitely knew what buttons to push. "Yes, but he knew. He gave me his blessing before he died, and I like to think it eased his mind at the end."

Lee Ann shot him a quick, startled glance then nodded. "I'm sure it did. You've been planning this."

"Since before you left for the city lights."

Agnes pulled a handkerchief out of her pocket and dabbed at her eyes. "This is so romantic."

"Reminds me of a romantic movie." Felicia smiled. "Sometimes those movies have strange twists in them."

Lee Ann just stared at Felicia as though she was trying to figure her out.

When everyone was seated, Gunther reached over and gave Lee Ann's hand a gentle squeeze. He was rewarded with a beautiful smile. His heart opened, and he wanted it all to be true. But it wasn't true, at least not for her. With that thought, his heart squeezed painfully.

"So, Lee Ann, I'm curious if you have a dress for the ball next week." Felicia pushed her plate away and leaned back in her chair. "If you don't I could take you shopping in town."

Dang it, she was up to something. Gunther had all but forgotten about the Dancing Under the Lights Ball they held yearly as a way to reach out to the community.

Lee Ann faltered for the barest second. Then a smile spread across her face. "I'm set, but thank you for the offer."

After dinner, they stood on the front porch and bid Felicia good night. Lee Ann smiled at him.

"It's such a beautiful night. Let's go for a walk," she suggested.

Gently, he took her hand and led her down the porch steps. They walked over to the horse pasture and watched a few of the mares. "I'm surprised to see Sabrina out there. Doesn't she usually go back to her stall at night?"

Lee Ann laughed. "If you can catch her, you can bring her in. She's decided she likes it better outside. Of course, we could always rope her and bring her in, but I think she'll be just fine for now. We'll reevaluate when the weather gets cold."

Her face glowed under the moonlight, and he couldn't have stopped even if he wanted to. He leaned down and his lips found her soft, sweet ones. He hesitated at her initial gasp but then he realized she was kissing him back. His instinct was to scoop her up and carry her off to a place where he could explore every inch of her. But he knew better. It was too soon, she was hurting too much.

So he kissed her until it became too uncomfortable for him. Then he slowly pulled away from her and stared into her eyes. They were full of happiness and wonder and what he wished was love.

"Whew, that was some kiss," he said.

Lee Ann nodded. "All that champagne went right to my head, I guess."

He highly doubted the champagne had anything to do with their kiss but he smiled. "We'd best be getting back." The walk wasn't long and he kissed her on the cheek as he said good-bye at the foot of the stairs. He waited as she walked up to the guest room. Then he slipped into his study for a shot of whiskey.

CHAPTER SEVEN

*L*ee Ann stared at herself in the mirror. The long black gown didn't leave much to the imagination. She should have insisted on a different dress but Gunther wanted her to wear this one. It was their annual Dancing Under the Lights Ball. She'd never been invited to go before, though she had watched from her window.

She'd watched her father shake one hand after another. He never danced. The women had always been finely dressed, but she never took much notice to what they wore exactly. She'd been busy trying to catch a glimpse of Gunther. It had been a game to her except for the last year she'd been at the ranch, when she had watched as he danced with every beautiful young woman in attendance. That night had been her deciding factor for leaving the ranch. She had known in that moment she wouldn't be able to take it if Gunther married another and obviously, no one had thought her old enough to attend the ball.

Her brown hair was swept up and she loved the way it looked but the dress…

"Lee Ann! Gunther asked me to escort you outside!" Woody yelled from outside her door.

"Coming!" She didn't have a wrap or a clutch purse at the main house. She hadn't given it much thought. She smiled, at least she had shoes that were pretty even if they did pinch her feet.

She opened the door and grinned. "Wow, Woody! Look at you! You'll make all the woman's hearts beat fast tonight."

He grinned back as he offered her his arm. "You're looking all kinds of good too. Gunther is anxious to have you by his side." They walked down the steps and outside. The field they used for parking was getting crowded. "I'm happy for you both. I know it's been a few weeks, but I haven't had a chance to tell you that."

All the felicitations were making her uncomfortable. She hated lying to everyone she cared about. Announcing their engagement hadn't made Felicia back off. In fact, it was as though she was up for the challenge of stealing Gunther away.

A dance floor had been set up in the yard, and the scent of barbecue filled the air. Tables had been set everywhere. It always struck her as funny to see white tablecloths on the ranch. People were sipping drinks and mingling. It might be fun after all.

She took her arm from Woody's and clasped her hands in front of her. What would Gunther think? Would he like the dress on her? Seeing a dress on a mannequin was vastly different than seeing it on a person.

He separated himself from the group of men he was talking to as she approached, and her mouth went dry. Jiminy Crickets! He was such a handsome man. His black suit, bolo tie, and shiny black boots only enhanced his good looks. Women would be drooling after him all evening.

He whistled. "Wow! Look at you! You are so lovely, you

take my breath away." He captured her hand, drew it to his lips and pressed a soft kiss to her knuckles.

She could get used to this pretending if it was all about compliments and smiles.

Heat rushed to her face. "Thank you. You look very nice yourself."

He walked down the steps and grabbed her hand. "I'm proud to have you by my side."

"How red is my face?" she murmured. "You need to lay off with the compliments."

He gave her an odd smile. "We'll have quite a showing tonight. My dad would have been pleased."

"Mine too. Should I take off the engagement ring?"

He stopped walking and stared at her. "Of course not. Let's get a drink and mingle."

She squeezed his hand. "I'm no good at mingling. I never say the right thing. Half the time they talk about things I don't care about and my mind drifts, and then they want my opinion. If anyone starts in about recipes, I'm going to scream."

Gunther's chuckle was loud and many heads turned their way. "We'll keep it short and sweet. After all, we'll have to greet each guest. That should take up half the night and the other half I plan to dance with you." He grinned at her. "I promise I won't ask you for a single recipe."

"Thank heavens for that!" She took the glass of champagne a waiter offered. "Let's get this done."

"Your father used to say that."

"I know."

The next few hours were pure hell for her. Shaking hands, getting kissed on her cheek, and making conversation with people she didn't know was unnerving. With each introduction she wondered if the person knew about her or if they'd seen her pictures. A few times, she tried to excuse herself but he knew. Gunther knew she wouldn't come back. He could always read her. The next wave of guests were the late comers, the ones who thought they were important enough to make an entrance. Unfortunately, this group was full of beautiful, young women. By comparison, she was dressed like a nun.

She'd never wanted to rip the hair off people's heads before, but now that was all she wanted to do. That and smudge the lipstick on all the pouty lips that happened their way. Instead, she grinned and bore it. She could do this. It was only one night, and she had Gunther to lean on.

One overdressed couple pushed their way in front of the receiving line. They reminded her of Barbie and Ken dolls. Gunther tensed, and Lee Ann had a bad feeling.

They approached and Gunther smiled. "Lee Ann, this is Roberto Perez and Kimberly Gleason."

Kimberly looked Lee Ann up and down before she frowned. "I don't see what all the fuss is about. Do you, Roberto?"

Lee Ann was stunned.

"She looks better without her clothes. Her assets need to be on display." He stared at her chest.

Before she knew it, Woody and Angus were pulling Gunther off Roberto. Roberto looked like he'd been kicked in the face by a mule.

"Leave. Now!" Gunther stood straight and proud until the couple was off his property. He held his handkerchief against his lip. "I apologize. Please continue with the party." He touched her cheek and nodded. "I'll be right back."

She downed the rest of the champagne in her glass in one gulp, and a waiter brought her a fresh one immediately. She'd lived here most of her life, but many of the guests weren't people she'd seen before. She wished she had a best friend besides Gunther. A female friend she could confide in. But she stood in a crowd of people feeling so very alone.

It didn't take long before she was being stared at. The pictures. She decided to go check on Gunther when a man stepped into her path. She gasped aloud. It was Kevin Burns. She took a step back, stumbling a bit.

He grabbed her upper arm and righted her. Then he pulled her onto the dance floor. Lee Ann willed herself to remain calm, but it was hard. He held her against his body, grabbing her rear end and kissing her neck.

"Shh, just dance. You don't want another incident here tonight, do you? Gunther probably lost some buyers already by his barbaric actions."

A hysterical laugh bubbled up inside of her until she couldn't keep it in any longer. "You don't identify with his barbaric actions? What the heck do you call beating a woman so badly she had to miss two weeks of work? I would call that barbaric—"

His repugnant lips closed over hers. She squirmed, but he held tight, and she didn't dare make him mad.

She sensed Gunther before she saw him. He looked outwardly calm but she knew better. "Miss Simpson, I think we have a few things to discuss. Excuse us, Mr. Burns." Gunther took her hand in a punishing grip and walked so fast she could barely keep up in her high heels.

She wanted to beg him to slow down, but there were people everywhere giving her condemning looks. Her heart sank, and a great emotional pain engulfed her. Kevin had gotten his revenge. He was probably sitting in his car outside the gates waiting for her to come out with a suitcase.

As soon as the office door closed, fear filled her. Gunther's eyes were filled with rage. He let go of her hand and she almost fell over. She grabbed onto one of the chairs in front of his desk and then sat down while her legs shook.

"How did you end up in Kevin's arms? Am I missing something? I thought you hated him?" He ran his hand over his face as pain filled his eyes. "I need the truth from you. Why was he here and why were you kissing him?"

"I didn't invite him. You must already know that. I don't understand why you're acting as though I did something wrong!"

"I'm not sure what was happening out there. I do know that everyone saw you. That man had no right to be on my property. Why didn't you just walk away when you saw him?"

Lee Ann's heart dropped. He obviously doubted her. It was too much to bear. Her life had been nothing but fear and doubt until recently. She hoped that she and Gunther... "I thought you knew me better than that. I can't stay where my integrity is in question. I've lived that way and I refuse to live that way again." She waited for his apology but it didn't happen.

She slid the ring off her finger and with shaking hands she put the ring on his desk. She stared at him waiting for him to ask her to stay and the longer she stared the more her heart broke. "I guess this is it then."

"I suppose so. I wanted to make the engagement real." He paused as though he was reining in his temper. "Figure out where you want to go. I'll have someone take you to the bus station in the morning." His fists were balled by his sides and his Adam's apple bobbed as he swallowed hard.

"I didn't invite him here. It's not what you think—"

"Right now I'm too mad to hear anything you have to say. Figure out where you want to go." He picked up the ring and put it in his pocket before he left slamming the door behind him.

Stunned, she sat there. What in heaven's name happened? Where could she go? How could she bear to leave? A fresh start would be good. Her father had left her a bit of money. Gunther was going to make the engagement real? As that thought struck, her heart shattered. A marriage between them would have never worked. He didn't trust her enough.

She went upstairs to her room and watched from the window. There were many women there to console Gunther. She couldn't watch anymore; it hurt too much. She slipped off her dress and opted for jeans, a T-shirt, and a pair of boots. Quietly, she left the house. She didn't dare saddle a horse so she walked to her father's grave.

As soon as she saw his grave marker, she burst into tears. This was where her best friend was. She'd never felt his loss so profoundly until now. The grief became unbearable. Rocking herself back and forth on the ground, she cried. Then she lay her head down next to the spot he was buried and fell asleep.

She woke up to the chatter of squirrels in the tree above her. She smiled briefly until grief took her. At least her head was a bit clearer this morning. She might not be able to get a job as a writer but she was darn good with horses. There had to be plenty of ranches around where she could get a job. Her dad always said that people who fell down had to pick themselves back up and keep going. Good advice.

She began to walk back to the house when she saw Gunther on his horse heading toward her. She couldn't face him, so she kept walking.

"Wait, Lee Ann," Gunther called.

Hope filled her. He was going to ask her to stay. She stopped and turned toward him. The sad expression on his face negated all her hopes. She took a deep breath and let it out slowly.

"Did you want something?" she asked.

"As soon as you're ready, I'll take you to the bus station." He turned his horse and rode away.

It was a mess of her own making. She never should have left the ranch in the first place. Really, who had she expected to hire a green writer?

He'd stood there smiling at her, asking her opinion of a page layout when he grabbed the back of her hair and then punched her hard in the gut. She doubled over unable to breath. He pulled her up by her hair and his sickly smile filled her with fear so great she froze. He hit her in the stomach again and when she went down, he kicked her over and over until there was nothing left for her to do but roll into a ball and try to protect her head.

She'd never felt such pain before, and the humiliation had been too much to bear. When she'd threatened to go to the police he had laughed at her. She defied him by leaving and he got his revenge. Hopefully she'd find a place where he'd never find her.

The door to the house was wide open. She cautiously approached not wanting to see Gunther but when she caught sight of Agnes, she calmed a bit.

"My dear, I'm so sorry about what happened. Everyone could tell you didn't want to dance with that man. Gunther will come around."

"I'm not even going to hope for such a miracle. The only man who never betrayed me was my father. I'm not believable or worthy of trust. My word counts for nothing. Sad but true. It's time to move on. I need a new slate. Gunther had more than enough women willing to console him last night." She let out a humorless laugh. "It's funny, I've lived here all my life, and the only friends I have are his friends. It's time to start my own life with my own friends and maybe someday I'll have my own family."

"Such brave words my courageous girl. My heart breaks for you. I can see the enormous amount of love you have for Gunther, and he feels the same for you."

"Agnes I know you're trying to help, but you're making me feel worse." A tear escaped and trailed down her cheek until she quickly wiped it away. "I'll let you know where I am once I'm settled."

"I'll have your things shipped once you get settled. You take care of yourself." They hugged, and Lee Ann didn't want to let go but she had no choice. A horn sounded.

"I guess that's for me." She grabbed a small bag and took one last look at the house she'd grown up in before heading outside.

It was a day filled with sunshine. The type of day that a person wouldn't expect anything bad to happen. She opened the truck door and got in. It was a great relief to see Woody behind the wheel. Then she closed the door and put her seat-belt on. Turning her head, she watched the scenery as they drove by. Her throat began to close and tears threatened but she bit the inside of her mouth and was able to stay the tears.

"Do you know where you'll go? Do you need money?" His voice was full of concern.

"No and no." She didn't even look at him. Relief flowed through her when they pulled up to the bus station. She jumped out of the truck and went inside.

CHAPTER EIGHT

our Months Later

Lee Ann smiled at the progress she'd made. She had found a family ranch in Oklahoma that needed someone experienced with horses. They wanted to build a horse breeding addition to their ranch but didn't know much about horses.

She worked for a wonderful family, The Cheney's. Elliot and Carol. They had twin four-year-olds, Constance and William. The pay wasn't great, but she had a room over the barn and all she could eat. She was safe, and that was all that mattered. She just wished her broken heart would mend. There wasn't a shortage of eligible cowboys around, but she just couldn't bring herself to date. The downside was she had too much time to think about Gunther.

He'd probably moved on. Maybe he'd married Felicia and gotten his bit of land. She sent Agnes her address but she didn't want her things sent; she just didn't have the will to open them. No one else had tried to contact her, and while she was relieved it also made her bitter. She wished she could hate Gunther. It would have been so much easier. But he haunted dreams and even when she lay in bed trying to sleep, she replayed their kisses again and again.

He was probably with Felicia now. That would serve him right. A quick smile spread across her face. This was her life now. It was time to make some friends and make it feel like home.

———

A FEW DAYS LATER, she was in the barn checking on some of the pregnant mares. It was all so peaceful except for the twins running around screaming, but even that made her smile. It had been such a struggle to get to this place where her heart wasn't constantly breaking. Sometimes life had other plans for people, and even though it hurt, that was just the way it was.

Sometimes there just wasn't no way to fix it. Her father often said those words. Now they filled her with strength and comfort. He was still watching over her, and he'd given her the tools to succeed in life. Work hard and work honest had been his advice. He'd been right; she was standing on her own two feet, working hard and honest, and she was enjoying that part of her life. One day at a time.

A piercing scream interrupted her thoughts and she ran toward it. To her dismay, William was on the ground writhing in pain. Constance ran to get her parents. His leg looked to be broken in more than one place. Glancing around, Lee Ann spotted the gopher hole. She immediately began to get his jeans off. She had no way of ripping them. William didn't think much of the idea but she succeeded without causing too much further pain. A bone stuck out of his skin and she immediately felt his foot for a pulse. There wasn't one.

She needed to reset the bones as best they could until the

ambulance came and get blood going to his foot before he lost it. The pain on his face hurt her.

"This is going to hurt, but it needs to be done. She quickly found two small branches she could use as splints. She then ripped off her T-shirt and using her teeth she managed to make strips she could tie to make the splints stay.

She sat back on her heels. This was going to hurt like hell and she had no one to hold William down. Taking a deep breath, she put her foot in Williams arm pit and pulled with all her might. She'd never forget the scream of pain from William but then he was silent. She sat back up and checked him. He'd passed out. She sighed deeply and then immediately tended to his leg. She finally got it splinted and to her relief his foot was turning back to a natural color.

Carol came running with tears streaming down her face. "How is he?"

"I think he'll be able to keep both his leg and foot. They'll resplint him once the ambulance gets here. He was in a lot of pain. Thankfully, he passed out."

Carol's eyes widened as she stared at Lee Ann. "Do you have medical training?"

"No, but my father was a ranch foreman, and I tended to many of the hands." This was not a tone of a grateful woman, and Lee Ann put her guard up.

"What did you mean by his foot? Are you claiming he might have lost it to a broken leg?" Carol cocked her brow. "Lee Ann, I think you're taking this opportunity to overstate your importance."

"I need to get a shirt." She turned and walked to the barn. What had just happened? One minute she was part of their family, and the next it sounded like she'd better be ready to pack her bags. She went to her quarters and put a clean shirt on. Unsure if she should go back down or not she decided to go. Her concern for William was real. Carol was probably just upset.

The cold hard stare she got from Carol upon her return made her stomach churn. William was still on the ground and instead of stroking his head or holding his hand, Carol just stared at Lee Ann. Where was Elliot? Surely, Carol had called him.

"I suppose this is as good a time as any," Carol said, her voice cold. "Your services are no longer needed. I'd appreciate it if you were off my property by the time we come back from the hospital."

Lee Ann's heart squeezed as her stomach dropped. "I'll need my pay."

Carol laughed. "I think Elliot serviced you enough. Think of that as your payment."

"What are you talking about?"

Carol shrugged. "The same thing the whole town is talking about. The naked pictures of you. I wouldn't have hired you if I had known you were a prostitute. Can you imagine my embarrassment when you and my husband are the subject *de jour*? Time for you to leave."

Stunned, Lee Ann shook her head. "I don't understand. I'll pack my things, but I'll need a ride."

"Find your own ride! Just leave!"

Lee Ann ran to the barn. She'd admired Carol, but she'd been so wrong. Carol hardly looked at her son the whole time her son had laid there. With tears flowing, Lee Ann packed her meager belongings

What had Elliot said when he was confronted? Didn't he deny anything happened? She only had two hundred and five dollars. It wouldn't get her far. She needed to contact her father's attorney. She'd never signed the papers for her inheritance. It had been too painful at first, and then she'd left Gunther's ranch too quickly, but now she had no choice.

Could she slip into town and out again without Gunther knowing? She laughed bitterly. He wouldn't care. It still boggled her mind how lies spread on the internet suddenly became truth. No one asked if it was true or asked what happened. It was more about hiding the pictures and her shame. But it wasn't really her shame; she'd done nothing wrong. Yet this would follow her for the rest of her life, and it hurt unbearably.

She didn't have a place to hole up and lick her wounds. She looked out the window at the sound of the ambulance and saw them load William into the back. By then Elliot was there holding Constance. Carol rode in the ambulance with their injured son.

Lee Ann sat at the window waiting for Elliot and his daughter to leave. He stood there for a long while staring at her window. Was that regret she saw on his face? It didn't matter. As soon as the coast was clear, she called a cab.

CHAPTER NINE

*G*unther sat on his front porch drinking his coffee in the predawn hours. He hadn't slept a full night since Lee Ann had left. The saturated hues of orange and yellow filled the sky, and he wished she was there to share it with him. He felt like a first class heel. He'd jumped to conclusions in his anger and he said so much he wished he could take back. He'd been furious with Burns and it spilled over to her. He was also mad at himself for not protecting her from Burn's attentions. He hadn't thought anything out when he asked her to leave. He didn't realize she'd take his heart with her.

He sighed. Lee Ann wanted nothing to do with him, and he didn't blame her. She'd been through so much and he was supposed to have had her back; that was what friends did. He'd wanted more than friendship, but that was never going to happen. If he were her, he wouldn't be forgiving either.

He'd been such a jerk. He had a permanent ache in his heart, and he knew it wouldn't go away. His only consolation was that Agnes knew where Lee Ann was and had told him she was fine living with a nice family on a ranch. Still, he worried. She was vulnerable and hurt and alone. His jaw tensed. What if she wasn't alone anymore?

He hadn't realized how much he'd banked on seeing her again. He'd looked forward to spending time with her, walking, talking, riding. But he'd thrown it away, and his heart was lonely for her. It was his fault, but there was no fixing it.

The front door squeaked as it opened. Agnes walked outside, coffee in hand and sat down. "Another night of no sleep?"

He hated the worried look in her eyes. "I slept just fine. I woke a bit early is all."

Her eyes narrowed before she nodded. He never could fool her.

"Life is full of curveballs, isn't it, Agnes?"

"Sometimes the curveballs are good." She took a sip of her coffee before she put her cup down on the wooden table. "I'm worried about her. She wrote to say she left her job and she'd let me know once she was settled but that was over a week ago. I know it's not a very long time but…"

"Where was she? Agnes, before you even think about it, you are not breaking her trust. She might be in trouble. Heck, knowing Lee Ann she is in trouble."

Agnes nodded and pulled a piece of paper out of her pocket. "This is the last address I had for her. It's a family ranch, and she was going to start a horse breeding program for them. I called asking about Lee Ann and if they knew where she went, but they just said she no longer worked there."

"Thanks for this." He stood and leaned over giving Agnes a kiss on her cheek. "You're one in a million." Her blush pleased him. "I'll get right on this." Determination replaced his smile as he walked to his office.

Lee Ann's former employers weren't very forthcoming on the phone until he threatened to go down there. He finally got Mrs. Cheney to tell him about an affair Lee Ann had with her husband and how she tried to harm her son William. Gunther didn't say anything but he was steaming mad by the time he hung up.

Lee Ann wasn't the affair type and she'd never harm a child. He hit his desk with his hand. If only he hadn't accused her of being with Kevin Burns, she'd still be here. This was his fault.

Unfortunately, he'd been blinded by his temper. He played right into Kevin's hands. He had to find her. Mrs. Cheney admitted she hadn't paid her. Inexcusable!

Where to start looking? He hopped on the internet and by the time he was done, he wanted to vomit. There was plenty about Lee Ann and none of it nice or true.

LEE ANN COLLECTED HER INHERITANCE. It was much more than she expected but not enough for her to be set for life. Next, she looked at property. If she could get land with a small house she could afford a few horses, and in a couple years she might have a profitable ranch. Of course, she'd have to run some cattle too at first to make enough money to live on.

She looked everywhere near Fort Worth, but the price for land was too high. Finally, she bought a junker of a truck and began to ride the dirt roads out away from the city. Land became more reasonably priced the farther out she went.

She saw a sign for sale by owner and stopped her truck. The house was a beat up trailer but it was the land that interested her. Pastures were already fenced and water pumps could be seen near each. She got out of her truck and knocked on the door.

An older gentleman answered and invited her in.

"Thanks, but I don't know you. I really wanted to walk the land if that would be fine with you, sir."

"The name is Longneck, just Longneck."

"I'm Lee Ann."

"Fine by me if you want to walk around. I don't get out much anymore and I haven't been able to tend to the place as I should." He sighed. "I have a son in Oklahoma who wants me to come live with his family. I resisted but now I think it's time. Stop on by when you're done. I'll put the coffee on."

She had a good feeling about Longneck. "I'd like that." She turned and began to walk the fence lines. He still owned at least a hundred head of cattle and nine horses. The grass was lush. The price would be too much even with the trailer falling apart. It would have been nice. She walked back and peeked into the barn. It was clean and well stocked with hay. His animals lived better than he did.

The door opened before she knocked. "Come on in, Lee Ann. Let's haggle." He held the door for her.

She climbed up the two rickety steps and walked inside. It was clean but beyond repair as far as she could tell. There were holes in the floor. She pretended nothing was wrong. After all, this was his home.

"Have a seat at the table. I'll grab the coffee." He grabbed two mugs and set them down on the table. "Sugar? I don't have cream."

"Black is just fine." Lee Ann smiled at him.

He poured the coffee and sat down across from her. "Are you representing a corporation?"

She shook her head.

"How about a land company or builders?"

She shook her head again. "I grew up on a wonderful ranch. I made a mistake and thought city living would be more glamorous but it wasn't. My dad is dead, and I just wanted to make a fresh start. I've been accused of things I haven't done."

"Stealing?"

She shook her head.

"Killin'?"

She shook her head. "It was nothing like that. It's embarrassing actually. My employer in the city took pictures of me through my window and put them on the internet. Everywhere I go those pictures surface and I end up jobless."

"Are you a woman of immoral character?"

"No, I've never…" Her face heated. "I really shouldn't talk about it with you. It only brings me shame." She stood. "Thank you for the coffee."

"Where you going?" He gestured for her to sit back down.

"What would you do with the land if it was yours?" He leaned in as if the answer was of the highest importance.

She smiled. "I plan on breeding horses and raising some cattle. Ranching is in my blood. My father was a ranch foreman, so I've learned a thing or two. I'm a hard worker and I never shirk my duties. If I have to work from sun up to sun down and then some, I'd do it. Owning land is a privilege that is getting too expensive for most people, including me. I'm only wasting your time. I'm just looking for a place to call home. A place no one can make me leave. I don't want to be the girl with pictures on the internet. I want to be a well-respected rancher. I believe if you nurture the land and animals, they nurture you back. My goodness I'm talking your ear off."

"No, not at all. I've had offers from land builders. Big money but I can't have my ranch cut up into lots. My family fought for generations for this land, and I was so sorry when my son didn't want to ranch. How much can you pay?"

"Not nearly as much as it's worth."

He squinted his right eye as though he was thinking. "Tell

you what. I could lease you the land. A life lease for you and your children etc. If you ever sell, the money goes to my heirs. Lord knows I don't need the money. I made a killing in the stock market plus the income from this place."

She furrowed her brow. "But the house is…well, it needs work."

Longneck laughed. "I have a nosey neighbor, Mrs. Jenkins, who thinks she can tell me what to do. I keep this trailer here to annoy her. I have another ready to be delivered next week. She'll be going north for the summer. I made the mistake in dating her for a while, and she tried to act like my mother. That was thirty years ago."

"I don't think I've heard of a life lease before."

Longneck shrugged. "That's for the lawyer to figure out. You can pay me one hundred dollars a month to start. I want you to put as much money as you have into this place. I knew my health was on a decline so I haven't purchased more cattle in a few years. I have a good friend who stops by and gets hard work done for me. I'll ask him to do the same for you."

Lee Ann stood and gave Longneck a big hug. "I think I may be dreaming. This is all too much."

"Sometimes all we need in life is a helping hand. Where are you staying? The Shady Room?"

"How did you know?"

He chuckled. "Only place around to stay. Tell Stella to put your room on my tab."

"I couldn't—"

"You can and you will. I'll have the lawyer draw up the papers and get that new trailer set for you. My dear, you've made this old man happy. Now go and enjoy your day."

Her mind was spinning as she drove to the motel. What if he was crazy and it was all a bad joke? She'd best use her time looking for another place.

CHAPTER TEN

*G*unther ran his hand over his weary face. He'd looked high and low and couldn't find any recent trace of Lee Ann. There was nothing after her cashing her inheritance check. She hadn't opened a bank account as far as he could find. It had been six months and he was ready to admit he might not see her again. She didn't want him to find her. It weighed hard on his heart.

He was as grouchy as a bear; even Woody avoided him when he could. The only good thing was Felicia had had enough of him and finally sold him the land. It should have made him happy but it really didn't. What good was it to have things if you have no one to share it with?

He walked out of his office and jammed his hat on his head. "I'm going to Longneck's," he called to Agnes.

"Tell him I said hello!" Agnes yelled from upstairs.

Gunther walked outside. The heat of the long summer was finally lifting, and it felt good. Lately he'd felt as though he just couldn't breathe. He climbed into his truck and started the drive to Longneck's ranch. It was about two hours out.

As he drove he checked out the other ranches and properties. Some were in disrepair and it stunned him that he hadn't known. He usually made the trip to Longneck's every six weeks but he said he had hired a hand. Gunther shook his head. He'd let his worries take over his life. Neighbors needed to take care of each other, and he made a mental note of which ones he needed to visit in the next few days. It seemed that people were always hesitant to ask for help. Usually it was a broken arm or some ranch accident that kept a man down for a few months.

Longneck had been a friend of his father's. A smarter man he'd never met but he was a bit eccentric. It was rumored he had a big fancy house up north and came down to ranch on land he'd owned forever, just to get away from his kids. Gunther shrugged. He was a good rancher, but Gunther didn't quite believe the big house story. Longneck's trailer had holes in the floor, and it was dubious that the shower worked right. He'd offered to take a look at it, but Longneck said he was having someone come out and fix it.

He smiled when the ranch came into view. It looked nicer than it ever had, and his eyes widened at the sight of the new trailer. Whomever he'd hired had been good for him. He didn't see Longneck's truck around but he turned into the driveway anyway. He saw movement in the barn and his heart nearly beat out of his chest.

"Lee Ann," he whispered.

He wasn't ready to see her. He backed out of the driveway and drove off. It was a cowardly act, but he'd panicked. He drove to the nearest parking lot and pulled in. Then he put the truck in park and just sat there. Maybe his eyes were playing tricks on him. He took a deep breath and shook his head. No. It was Lee Ann. How did she know Longneck? All this time she'd been only two hours away, and he hadn't been able to find her.

His eyes dampened in relief that she was okay. He hadn't realized just how afraid for her he was. His hands shook as he grasped the steering wheel. She was just down the street he could go and talk to her. He could say he was checking on Longneck...

His heart refused to slow, and he felt as though he'd run a marathon. This is what he'd been waiting for and here he sat like a frightened child. What if she didn't want to see him? He'd treated her so badly.

No, he couldn't face her just yet. He didn't know what to say. He'd just drive home and give Longneck a call. It was the easy way out, but he couldn't bring himself to see her and have her turn him away. He put the truck in drive and went back home.

LEE ANN SAT under the awning in the front of her place thinking about the truck that had ventured onto her property. Maybe it hadn't been Gunther. She shook her head. No, it had been, and he'd sped away. She quickly dashed away her tears with the back of her hand. Whatever might have been was in the past. She'd often thought about how she'd act if she saw him again. She'd dreamed about his wide spread arms and how she'd run into them. To be in his strong embrace again would be heaven.

She never ever thought he'd turn and go the other way. Her heart squeezed painfully, and her head began to ache. Someday, perhaps she'd find someone. Gunther had been the one who'd thrown her away, and she couldn't figure out why she still loved him. Unfortunately, she could see it all from his point of view. He loved her that much she knew. He had his pride, though he could have asked her about Kevin. He took it all at face value and it broke his heart.

He hadn't deserved an explanation at the time. He should have believed in her, he should have trusted her. But Kevin sure had put on a nasty show of dancing so intimately with her. Frankly, she couldn't be certain she would not have reacted the same way Gunther had.

Swallowing hard, she got herself up and went back to the barn to finish mucking out stalls. She had a lot of sleepless nights in her future.

Two weeks later

"Spill it!" Agnes put her hands on her hips and stared Gunther down. "You've been like a wounded grizzly ever since you got back from Longneck's ranch. Did you two have a fight?"

"No we didn't." He wiped his mouth with his napkin and stood up. "I have work to do."

"Did you see Lee Ann?" Her voice was a bit gentler.

He narrowed his eyes and stared at her. "You knew she was there? The whole time?"

Agnes nodded and opened her mouth, perhaps to explain, but he didn't want to hear it. He stormed out the door. His heart twisted, and a lump formed in his throat. He needed to blow off some steam before he hurt someone. He walked behind the barn and started chopping wood.

How could Agnes have known and not tell him? Heck, he thought of her as a mother and she... Were all women the same? Did they all betray men? His torment refused to subside. Damn Kevin Burns to hell and back! He put the ax down sat on the ground next to the chopping block.

He raised his gaze up to the sky. It was cloudless, well

almost. There was a lone cloud, and sadness washed over him. Would he forever be a lone cloud? He shook his head. His heart relaxed a bit. He was certain of her love. It was there in each glance, every touch and in her soft words. Why hadn't he seen it while she was here?

Inviting Kevin wasn't something Lee Ann would do. She was clearly afraid of the man. He took off his Stetson and slapped it against his knee, and then stuffed it back on his head. It was he who'd betrayed *her*. All this time he'd blamed her and that was his fault. He was too hardheaded for his own good. His damn pride had gotten in the way of reason, and he'd hurt the only woman he'd ever love.

He got up went into the house, took a shower, and left without saying a word to Agnes. He didn't want anyone to know if he failed, again. He nodded as he drove. He'd visited his neighbors one by one and helped those in need. At least he'd done something right.

He swallowed hard. He still didn't have any idea of what he was going to say to her. She might not even want to talk to him, and he wouldn't blame her. The closer he got the more nervous he became.

He turned into the driveway and looked around, but he didn't see her. Stepping out of his truck, he noticed how serene everything around him felt. Peaceful and at peace, in stark contrast to the upended emotions that churned within him. He refused to let their love pass them by but he still didn't have a clue as what to say.

He felt her gaze on him before he turned. She looked lovely in jeans and a sky-blue T-shirt. She wore a light tan Stetson and it looked great on her. Her emotions played over her face. He saw surprise, hope, anger and sadness but best of all he saw love.

Her half smile didn't bode well. "I wasn't sure I'd see you again," she said.

"I've been looking for you since the day you left. I was so angry and I wasn't thinking straight." He drank in the sight of her. What if she sent him packing? "I saw you here a few weeks ago and I should have stopped and said hello."

"Why didn't you?" His stomach dropped at her cold tone.

He shifted from one foot to the other. "I didn't know what to say, and I took the coward's way out. I've been kicking myself ever since."

"And you have something to say now?" She stared hard at him, and he knew his next few words would dictate his future.

"I was so wrong and harsh and stupid. I didn't think I just acted, and I let my pride get in my way. When I saw Burn's hands and lips on you, I lost all rational thought. I was insanely jealous. I never should have passed judgment on you. You're the sweetest, kindest, honest woman I know, and why I didn't remember that in time, I'll never know. I don't know if you can ever forgive me. I don't forgive myself, so I really don't expect you to." He ran out of words and stood there awkwardly just looking at her.

"I'm in a good place now. I've got a lifetime lease on this land, and I'm making something of my life. It's only been a few months, but I feel as though I've made great strides. The feeling of accomplishment is hard to beat." She leaned forward and studied him closely. "You know Longneck, don't you?"

"Yes, he's been a mentor to me since my father passed."

She tilted her head. "You didn't have anything to do with Longneck being so kind to me did you?"

He couldn't help the grin that spread over his face. "No, if he was kind, that was all you. He'd had plenty of offers for the place but he kept telling me he was waiting for the right person. I guess he found her." He cleared his throat. "I'd love to see all the improvements if you're so inclined.

Hope blossomed at her big smile. He followed her around the ranch and listened intently to everything she had to say. She was one heck of an impressive woman.

"You know what you're doing and then some. Longneck chose wisely."

Lee Ann blushed. "Come on up to the house. I bet it looks a sight better than the last time you visited with Longneck."

―――――――

HER HANDS SHOOK as she led Gunther to her trailer. The whole day had been nerve racking. It felt so right to have him there with her, talking about the ranch. She was no longer the little girl. He treated her with respect and from the way his brow rose from time to time she impressed him.

"Come on in. I have some sweet tea for us." She walked in first and the heat from his body warmed her. "Have a seat."

He turned in a circle before he sat at the table. "Wow! This *is* an improvement."

"Yes I can't see the ground when I'm in here, and the shower has hot water." She put two glasses on the table. "How's Agnes?"

"I'm not talking to her."

Her jaw dropped. "What could she have done so terrible that you won't talk to her?"

"She knew where you were and didn't tell me." He gave her a sheepish grin.

"I asked her not to. I'm not your problem. You don't need to look out for me. You're free to live your life." She stared at her glass. Her words didn't match what was in her heart.

"What if I want you in my life?" He reached over and took her hand in his.

"We'll always be friends. Heck we grew up together. We

91

have history." His hand was so much bigger than hers. So masculine and strong.

"There is that. I was thinking about something a little more like a relationship."

She widened her eyes as she gazed at him. "Brother and sister?"

"That wasn't what I was thinking." He smiled.

"Friends without benefits?"

He laughed. "I've never heard the without part before. I've heard of friends *with* benefits."

"Then I'd have to say no." Remaining aloof took all her energy.

"That wasn't what I meant either. I love you, Lee Ann, and not like a sister or a girl to use or not use. Without you, part of me is missing, a huge part of me. I'm as sorry as I can be about the accusations I made."

A lump formed in her throat. "So, what is it you want? I'm not up for games."

"No games. I want you. I want you to spend your life with me. I want you by my side as we work the ranch. I want to see your face across from me at the dinner table. I want to see the sunshine on your face right before you wake up. I want to be able to take you into my arms and kiss you. I want to be able to call you my wife."

Her breath caught in her throat.

He groaned and stood. "I'm pushing too fast."

Lee Ann stood toe to toe with him. She took both of his hands in hers and met his gaze. "I love you too. It's been hell since I left. I won't lie. I wished you'd fall on your head and regain your senses. If we do this, we do it our way. No Felicia or Kevin or anyone else outside our circle making trouble. The pictures haunt me everywhere I go. My last employer accused me of sleeping with her husband. She heard rumors about me and the pictures and assumed." Her body relaxed when she saw there wasn't an ounce of suspicion in his eyes. "Agreed?"

He pulled her into his arms and rocked her back and forth. It was the comfort she'd sought all these months. His body was so hard and muscled against hers but the place right over his heart was soft for her to lay her head on. He stroked her back up and down. Tears flowed but she just let them. They were cleansing tears.

Slowly he released her and kissed away her tears before he took her lips with his. He groaned in pleasure as they deepened the kiss, and her heart soared. She didn't want things to go too far, so she stepped back. "I've never…you know, and I'd like to wait for my wedding night if I ever have one."

"You'll have one." He sounded incredibly sure. "You didn't like any of the other boys at school?"

"No, I ate my heart out watching you date all the pretty girls. There has never been anyone else for me."

Gunther stoked her cheek. "You amaze me. I guess I'll have to apologize to Agnes. I did act like a heel. I've spent so many sleepless nights worried about you these last six months."

"Me too. I missed you and I was nursing a broken heart. Gunther I want you to be absolutely sure you want to be with me. I couldn't take my heart shattering over you again."

He pressed his forehead against hers. "Marry me, Lee Ann. Be my wife and partner in all things. Let me love you forever."

Emotions over took her and she couldn't get any words out. She nodded and reached up, pulled his head down and kissed him again. She let go and smiled. Suddenly she laughed. "You have the ring with you, don't you?"

He chuckled. "As a matter of fact I do." He fished it out of his pocket and got down on one knee. "Lee Ann Simpson, will you marry me?"

She'd never seen his eyes so full of love before. "Of course I will." He slid the ring on her finger.

"You're coming home with me for a real celebration."

"I can't." She gestured around them. "The animals."

Gunther nodded. "I'll help you get them taken care of then we'll go. I'll bring you back later tonight."

A gasp slipped out. "It's a two-hour trip."

He hugged her again. "You're worth it."

EPILOGUE

 *wo months later*

"LEE ANN, HOLD STILL," Agnes admonished as she put flowers in Lee Ann's hair.

Lee Ann studied herself in the mirror, surprised to see a confident woman looking back at her. She glanced down at her engagement ring and smiled. Her heart felt so filled with love it almost overwhelmed her.

"Yep, you have that special glow about you," Agnes said as she took a step back and gazed at Lee Ann.

Lee Ann's face heated. "I'm not pregnant, if that's what you think."

Agnes' laugh started as a low rumbled until she was laughing so hard she needed to grab a tissue to wipe her eyes. "You have the glow of *love* about you. I know you're—well I know you couldn't be pregnant. Your parents would have been so proud of you. You've had to weather a lot in the last year, but you came out of it a strong woman who can be an equal partner to that rascal Gunther. I've never seen him happier."

Lee Ann smiled and twirled around in a circle, checking out her white dress in the mirror. It was fancier than she'd wanted, but Gunther'd insisted. What she loved most about it was the lace. It was in a pattern of a rose, and it covered most of her dress. Agnes was right. Lee Ann's parents would have been proud of her. She smiled to herself. She was proud of herself for sticking to her morals. It would have been easier to let Kevin Burns have his own way. It had taken all of her strength and courage to get through it all, and yet, she had come through.

With a few calls to the right people by a number of Kevin's other victims, he had been black listed from working in the publishing world by the corporate heads who hadn't wanted any further scandals. She'd have thought the news would have pleased her, but she didn't care. She was just grateful the threats were over.

"It's almost time," Agnes said with excitement in her voice.

Lee Ann gazed out the window and laughed when she spotted Gunther standing by the minister pulling at his collar. He was a top button undone type of man. All the ranch hands were there as was Longneck.

Longneck thought her idea of running a ranching program for disabled kids was remarkable. They'd been able to get the right couple to run it. Right now, they were putting in ramps and other things to make the whole place accessible to all.

She walked down the stairs and to the front door. She stood there for a moment staring at Gunther. He was such a handsome, strong, kind man. She said a quick prayer for happiness for them. His eyes were full of appreciation as she walked down the aisle. It was as though they only had eyes for each other.

A tear trailed down her face when he put the wedding ring on her finger. He'd wanted a glitzy band with inset diamonds, but she had insisted on something a bit more humble. A ring to match her engagement ring. When they kissed, she felt electrified and wished the feeling would never go away. She'd never been happier.

Halfway through the reception, Gunther tugged at her hand. "Come on, I want to go somewhere."

She readily took his hand and followed him to the stream where the bench they'd made as kids was. "You're crazy! Why are we here?" She laughed.

"I want a redo," he said his eyes full of mischief.

"A redo?"

"As I remember, our first kiss was a bit of a disaster, with you having cooties and all. I thought we'd try it again."

Oh, how she adored him. "It sounds like a fine idea." She squealed as he pulled her forward and put his arms around her.

They stared into each other's eyes for what seemed like forever before he leaned down and put his firm masculine lips against hers. He kissed her deeply and soundly until her lips were tingling and slightly swollen. "How was that?"

"I'm waiting to see if you wipe it off."

His brow furrowed. "Wipe it off?"

"You know, the cooties!" Filled with joy, she laughed loudly.

"No cooties," he murmured. Then his expression grew serious. "Lee Ann, I love you with everything within me. I'm forever yours."

THE END

I'm so pleased you chose to read I'm Forever Yours, and it's my sincere hope that you enjoyed the story. I would appreciate if you'd consider posting a review. This can help an author tremendously in obtaining a readership. My many thanks. ~ Kathleen

ABOUT THE AUTHOR

Sexy Cowboys and the Women Who Love Them...
Finalist in the 2012 and 2015 RONE Awards.
Top Pick, Five Star Series from the Romance Review.
Kathleen Ball writes contemporary and historical western
romance with great emotion and
memorable characters. Her books are award winners and
have appeared on best sellers lists including: Amazon's Best
Seller's List, All Romance Ebooks, Bookstrand, Desert
Breeze Publishing and Secret Cravings Publishing Best
Sellers list. She is the recipient of eight Editor's Choice
Awards, and The Readers' Choice Award for Ryelee's
Cowboy.
Winner of the Lear diamond award Best Historical Novel-
Cinders' Bride
There's something about a cowboy

facebook.com/kathleenballwesternromance

twitter.com/kballauthor

instagram.com/author_kathleenball

Oregon Trail Dreamin'

We've Only Just Begun

A Lifetime to Share

A Love Worth Searching For

So Many Roads to Choose

The Settlers

Greg

Juan

The Greatest Gift

Love So Deep

Luke's Fate

Whispered Love

Love Before Midnight

I'm Forever Yours

Finn's Fortune

Made in United States
Orlando, FL
22 September 2022

22694269R00059